He wasn't kissing her—she was kissing him. But maybe the delineation was blurring.

Maybe they were simply kissing. A man and a woman and a need as primeval as time itself.

Pippa.

His defences were disappearing, crumpling at the touch of her loveliness, in the aching need of her sigh, in the heat of their bodies. He was kissing in return, demanding as well as giving, his mouth plundering, searching her sweetness, glorying in her need as well as his own.

Pippa.

She was like no woman he'd ever touched. His body was reacting without control. She was stripping him bare, exposing parts of himself he'd never known he had—parts hidden behind barriers he'd built up with years of careful self-restraint.

Where was the self-restraint now?

Certainly not with Pippa.

THE DOCTOR & THE RUNAWAY HEIRESS

BY
MARION LENNOX

First published in Great Britain 2011
by Mills & Boon, an imprint of Harlequin (UK) Limited.
Large Print edition 2012
Harlequin (UK) Limited, Eton House,
18-24 Paradise Road, Richmond, Surrey TW9 1SR

© Marion Lennox 2011

ISBN: 978 0 263 22426 9

Harlequin (UK) policy is to use papers that are
natural, renewable and recyclable products and made
from wood grown in sustainable forests. The logging
and manufacturing process conform to the legal
environmental regulations of the country of origin.

Printed and bound in Great Britain
by CPI Antony Rowe, Chippenham, Wiltshire

Marion Lennox is a country girl, born on an Australian dairy farm. She moved on—mostly because the cows just weren't interested in her stories! Married to a 'very special doctor', Marion writes Medical™ Romances, as well as Mills & Boon® Romances. (She used a different name for each category for a while—if you're looking for her past Mills & Boon Romances, search for author Trisha David as well.) She's now had 75 romance novels accepted for publication.

In her non-writing life Marion cares for kids, cats, dogs, chooks and goldfish. She travels, she fights her rampant garden (she's losing) and her house dust (she's lost). Having spun in circles for the first part of her life, she's now stepped back from her 'other' career, which was teaching statistics at her local university. Finally she's reprioritised her life, figured out what's important, and discovered the joys of deep baths, romance and chocolate. Preferably all at the same time!

Recent titles by the same author:

CITY SURGEON, SMALL TOWN MIRACLE*
A BRIDE AND CHILD WORTH WAITING FOR**
ABBY AND THE BACHELOR COP†
MISTY AND THE SINGLE DAD†

*Mills & Boon® Medical™ Romance
***Crocodile Creek*
†Mills & Boon® Romance

These books are also available in eBook format from www.millsandboon.co.uk

CHAPTER ONE

DR RILEY CHASE was bored. It was his third night in a row with no action, and Riley was a man who lived on little sleep. His medico-legal bookwork was up to date. He was on his third coffee. He'd even defeated the crossword.

He was checking his email for the tenth time when his radio crackled to life.

Two messages in twenty seconds. One was announcing the arrival of a daughter he'd never met, the other was a suicide.

It was enough to make a man spill his coffee.

Only the headlines of Britain's gossip magazines were stopping her drowning.

'Heiress Suicides!'

Pippa was surrounded by blackness, by cold and by terror. Any minute now something would attack her legs. Maybe it already had—she could hardly feel anything below her waist. The cold was bone-numbing. She was past exhaustion, and there was only one thing holding her up.

'Phillippa Penelope Fotheringham, heiress to the Fotheringham Fast Food fortune, suicides after jilting.'

She would not give Roger the satisfaction of that headline.

'Are we sure it's suicide?' Riley was staring intently down at the blackened sea, feeling more and more hopeless.

'Jilted bride.' Harry Toomey, pilot for New South Wales North Coast Flight-Aid, was guiding the helicopter through parallel runs from the cliff. Harry, Riley and Cordelia, the team's Flight-Aid nurse, were searching north from Whale Cove's swimming beach. Grim experience told them this would be where a body would be swept.

'Do we have a name?' Riley said through his headset.

'Phillippa Penelope Fotheringham.'

'That's a mouthful.' Their floodlight was sweeping the water's surface, but the sea was choppy, making it hard to see detail. Detail like a body. 'Do we know how long she's been missing?'

'Five hours. Maybe longer.'

'Five hours!'

'There was a party on the beach that went till late,' Harry said. 'Kids everywhere. When they left, one of the security guys noticed an abandoned bundle of clothes. Plus a purse, complete with ID and a hotel access card. She could have been in the water since dusk, but we're assuming later, when it was good and dark.'

'Five hours is about three hours too long for a happy ending.'

Harry didn't bother replying. The crew knew the facts. The worst part of this job was pulling suicides out of the water. The jumpers were the worst—there was no coming back when you went over cliffs around here—but almost as bad were those who swam out from the beach knowing they couldn't get back. Desperate people. Desperate endings.

'So how do we know she just didn't have a good time at the party?' Riley demanded. 'She could have ended up back in someone else's hotel room.'

But even as Riley suggested it he knew it was unlikely. The police had called them in, and the cops around here knew their stuff.

'Logic,' Harry said, bringing the chopper round for the next pass. 'She's thirty-one, about ten years older than the party kids. She's staying at the Sun-Spa Resort, in the honeymoon suite no less. The cop who went to the hotel found her passport in the safe. She's English, and when he phoned the contact number in London, her parents had hysterics. It seems her wedding went up in smoke and our Phillippa fled to Australia with a broken heart. Alone. She arrived late. She booked into her honeymoon hotel with no wedding ring, no groom, and we can assume a decent dose of jet lag. Lethal combination. She headed for the beach, dumped her clothes and out she swam.'

'He's not worth it,' Riley muttered, feeling worse. Any minute now they'd find her. They usually did.

He was a doctor. He wasn't supposed to do this.

But, yeah, he was, he thought grimly. This was his choice. He, Harry and Cordelia did routine work, clinics in Outback settlements, flying in and out at need, but they also took Search and Rescue shifts. Sometimes it was incredibly satisfying, saving people from their own stupidity. Sometimes, though, like now...

Sometimes it was the pits.

Phillippa Penelope Fotheringham.

'Where are you, sweetheart?' After this time he knew they were searching for a body, but it was still incredibly important to find her. The parents could bury her, could grieve, could know exactly what had happened.

'So what was happening when the call came in?' Harry asked.

'What do you mean?'

'Who's Lucy?'

'You read my email?'

'Of course I did,' Harry said, unabashed. Harry was a highly skilled pilot, good-humoured and big-hearted, but his downside was an insatiable nose for gossip. 'You took thirty seconds to put your gear on, and you didn't supply alternative reading material. So someone called Lucy's coming on Friday and can you please put her up. You going to tell us who Lucy is?'

Riley thought of all the things he could say. *Mind your own business. A friend. Nobody important.* Maybe it was the grimness of the night, the tragedy playing out beneath the chopper, but in the end he couldn't bring himself to say anything but the truth.

'My daughter.'

My daughter.

The two words resonated through the headset, sounding…terrifying. He'd never said those words out loud until now.

He'd never had reason to say them.

'You're kidding us,' Harry breathed, turning into the next sweep. They were over the cliff now, momentary time out while Harry centred the machine for the next run; checking bearings so they weren't covering sea that had already been searched. 'Our solitary Dr Chase... A daughter! How old?'

'Eighteen.'

'Eighteen!' Riley could almost hear Harry's mental arithmetic. Cordelia was staring at him like he'd grown an extra head, doing maths as well.

'You're, what, thirty-eight?' Harry breathed. 'A daughter, eighteen years back. That's med student territory. Man, you've kept her quiet.'

He had. Mostly because he hadn't known she existed. Three months ago he'd received an email, sent via the Search and Rescue website.

Are you the Dr Riley Chase who knew my mother nineteen years ago?

Names. Dates. Details. A bombshell blasting into his carefully isolated existence.

And then nothing. No matter how desperately he'd tried to make contact, there'd been no word. Until tonight.

I'm arriving on Friday. Could you put me up for a few days?

But he couldn't afford to think about Lucy now. None of them could. The chopper was centred again. He went back to studying the waves, grimly silent, and Harry and Cordelia did the same.

Despite the bombshell Riley had just dropped, every sense was tuned to the sea. Harry was a flippant, carefree bachelor. Cordelia was a sixty-year-old dog breeder with a head cold. Riley was a man who'd just been landed with a daughter. Tonight though, now, they were three sets of eyes with only one focus.

Phillippa Penelope Fotheringham…

'Come on,' Riley muttered into the stillness. 'Give yourself up.'

The floodlight from their little yellow chopper, a Squirrel AS350BA—the best in the business, according to Harry—kept right on sweeping the surface of the night sea.

There was nothing but blackness. Nothing, nothing and nothing.

'Where are you?' Riley asked, but he was talking to himself.

Nothing.

There were lights. The mists cleared for a moment—the fog of fear and cold and fatigue—and let her see further than the next wave.

There were floodlights beaming out from the

cliffs, but they were so far out of her reach they might as well be on the moon.

She could see a helicopter moving methodically over the water. Was it searching for her? Had someone found her clothes?

It was a long way south. Too far.

Was it coming closer?

'Just hold on,' she told herself, but her body was starting to shut down.

She couldn't feel her feet at all. She couldn't feel anything.

She was treading water. Up and down. Up and down. If she stopped she'd slip under.

A wave slapped her face and made her splutter.

'I will not give Roger the satisfaction,' she muttered, but her mutter was under her breath. To speak was impossible. Her teeth were doing crazy things. She was so cold…

'I will not be a jilted bride. I will not die because of Roger.' It was a mantra, said over and over.

The helicopter turned.

It was still too far south. So far.

'I will not…'

'If it's suicide she'll definitely be dead by now and probably slipping under.'

'We all know that,' Harry said. 'But it doesn't stop us looking.'

'No, but...' Riley was speaking more to himself than to Harry. 'As a last resort let's think sideways.'

'What?'

The crew hadn't spoken for what seemed hours. They'd swept the expected tidal path and found nothing. Riley's words had tugged Cordelia and Harry out of their intense concentration, but Harry sounded as hopeless as Riley felt.

'I'm thinking,' Riley said.

'So think away. It's gotta be more useful than what we're doing now.'

Riley thought a bit more and then put it in words. 'Okay. If our Phillippa was a normal tourist with no intention to suicide... What time did she get to the hotel?'

'Around seven-thirty.'

'Let's say she's jet lagged, tired and hot. She walks out to the balcony and the sea looks great. She might take an impulsive dip at dusk. Eightish, maybe? The lifesavers would have long gone home, but it's not so dark that the water's lost its appeal. If she got into trouble at dusk, no one might see.'

'The party started on the beach at ten,' Harry said, hopelessness giving way to thought. 'No one noticed the clothes before then. We're working on search parameters based on an entry at ten at the earliest.'

'Sunday night. The beach was busy. One bundle of clothes might well go unnoticed. An entry at eight, she'd be a lot further north by now. And if it was a mistake she'll be fighting.'

'Her mother's sure she's suicidal.'

'How much does your mother know about you?' Riley demanded.

'I'd hate to imagine,' Cordelia retorted—which was a lot of speech for Cordelia. She was quiet at the best of times, but tonight her head cold was making her miserable.

There was a moment's pause while they all thought this through. Then: 'I guess it's worth a shot,' Harry said, and hit the radio. 'Assuming an eight o'clock entry,' he asked Bernie in their control room, 'can you rework the expected position?'

They did two more unsuccessful sweeps before Bernie was back with a location.

'Half a kilometre north and closer to shore,' Harry relayed. 'Let's go.'

It'd be so easy to slip under.
There will be no headlines. Not.
She was so tired.

The light. Had it turned? Was it coming?

She was imagining it. Her mind was doing funny, loopy things. The stars, the fluorescence of the waves and the roar of the sea were merging into a cold, menacing dream.

If this light wasn't really in her head she should raise her hand. If she could summon the energy. She could just…

Maybe not.

She must.

'Something.'

The Squirrel banked and turned almost before Riley barked the word. Harry was good.

So was Riley. His eyes were the best in the business. But still…the water was so choppy. They were in by the cliffs; any closer and they'd be victims themselves.

'Sure?' Harry snapped.

'No. Ten back. Five left. Hover.'

They hovered. The floodlight lit the water. The downdraught caused the water to flatten.

There…

'Got it,' Cordelia snapped.

They both had it. And what's more… There was a hand, feebly raised.

'She's alive,' Riley said, and he didn't try to keep

the exultation from his voice. 'How about that? Suicide or not, it seems our bride's changed her mind. Hold on, Phillippa Penelope Fotheringham, we're coming.'

The light...the noise... It was all around her. She couldn't think.

She also could no longer make her feet tread water.

A shadow was over her. Someone was yelling.

She was so tired.

Do not slip under. Do not.

Please.

Something was sliding into the water beside her. *Someone.*

She was too weak to clutch but she didn't need to. Arms were holding her. Just...holding.

Another human.

She was safe. She could let go. She had to let go. She could slip into the darkness and disappear.

'Don't you give up on us now, Phillippa Penelope Fotheringham,' someone growled. 'I've got you.'

She made one last effort. One massive effort because this was really, really important.

'I am not marrying Roger,' she managed. 'My choice, not his. And my name is not Phillippa. I'm Pippa.'

CHAPTER TWO

THERE were sunbeams on her bedcover. She woke and the sheer wonder of sunlight on linen was enough to make her want to cry.

Someone was standing at the end of her bed. Male. With a stethoscope.

She was in hospital?

Of course. The events of the night before came surging back—or maybe only some of the events, because there seemed to be gaps. Big gaps.

Water. Dark. Terror.

Then in the water, someone holding her, yelling at her, or maybe they were yelling at someone else.

Someone fastening her to him. Large, male, solid.

'You're safe. You don't need to hold on. I have you.'

Noise, lights, people.

Hospital.

'Hi,' the guy at the end of the bed said. 'I'm Dr Riley Chase. Welcome to the other side.'

The other side.

She surveyed the man talking to her with a certain degree of caution. He was…gorgeous. Tall, ripped and, after the nightmare of last night, reassuringly solid.

Beautifully solid.

She took time to take him in. Detail seemed important. Detail meant real.

His face was tanned and strongly boned. His deep blue eyes were crinkled at the edges. Laughter lines? Weather lines? Weather maybe. His near black hair—a bit unkempt, a bit in need of a cut—showed signs of sun-bleaching. That'd be from weather. He was wearing cream chinos. His short-sleeved shirt was open at the throat—this guy was definitely ripped—and his stethoscope was hanging from his top pocket.

Welcome to the other side?

Gorgeous fitted the *other side* description, she decided. Doctors didn't.

'Doctors aren't in my version of heaven,' she said, trying her voice out. She was vaguely surprised when it worked. Nothing felt like it should work this morning.

'It's definitely heaven,' he said, smiling a wide, white smile that made him look friendlier—and more heart-stoppingly gorgeous—than any doctor she'd ever met. 'In the other place the pillows are lumpy and we're big on castor oil and leeches.'

'And here?' she managed.

'Not a leech in sight, we reserve our castor oil for emergencies and there are two pillows for every bed. And because you were soggy the angels have decreed you can have more.' He waved an expansive hand around her not-very-expansive cubicle. 'Luxury.'

She smiled at that. She was in a two-bed cubicle that opened out into the corridor. The nurses' station was on the other side, giving whoever was at the station a clear view of her bed. Luxury?

'And heaven also means your medical care's totally free,' he added. 'Especially as your documents say you have travel insurance.'

Her documents?

There was enough there to give her pause. To make her take her time about saying anything else. She looked at Dr Riley Chase and he gazed calmly back at her. She had the impression that he had all the time in the world.

'Dr Chase?' a female voice called to him from the corridor. Maybe he didn't have all the time in the world.

'Unless it's a code blue I'm busy,' he called back. He tugged a chair to her bedside and straddled it, so he was facing her with the back of the chair between them. She knew this trick. She often wished she could use it herself but it was a guy thing. Guy thing or not, she appreciated it now. It gave the impression of friendliness, but it wasn't overly familiar. She needed a bit of distance and maybe he sensed it.

'You're on suicide watch,' he said bluntly. 'We have a staff shortage. Are you planning on doing anything interesting?'

She thought about that for a bit. Felt a bit angry. Felt a bit stupid.

'We're struggling with priorities,' he said, maybe sensing her warring emotions. Feeling the need to be apologetic. 'Olive Matchens had a heart attack last night. She's a nice old lady. We're transferring her to Sydney for a coronary bypass but until the ambulance is free I'd like a nurse to stay with her all the time. Only we need to watch you.'

'I don't need to be watched.'

'Okay, promise I have nothing to worry about?' He smiled again, and his smile... Wow. A girl could wake up to that smile and think it had been worth treading water for a night or more or more to find it. 'You need to know you're at risk of that cod liver oil if you break your promise,' he warned, and his smile became wicked. Teasing.

But there was seriousness behind his words. She knew she had to respond.

'I wasn't trying to do anything silly.' She tried to sound sure but it came out a whisper.

'Pardon?'

'I was not trying to suicide.' Her second attempt came out loud. Very loud. The noises outside the cubicle stopped abruptly and she felt like hauling her bedclothes up to her nose and disappearing under them.

'Your mother's frantic. She's on her way to Heathrow airport right now,' Dr Chase told her. 'With someone called Roger. Their plane's due to leave in two hours unless I call to stop them.'

Forget hiding under the bedclothes. She dropped her sheet and stared at him in horror. 'My mother and Roger?'

'They sound appalled. They know you're safe, but you've terrified them.'

'Excellent.'

'That's not very—'

'Kind? No, it's not. My mother still wants me to marry Roger.'

'This sounds complicated,' he said, sounding like he was beginning to enjoy himself. Then someone murmured something out in the corridor and he glanced at his watch and grimaced. 'Okay, let's give you the benefit of the doubt, and let Roger and Mum sweat for a bit. What hurts?'

'Nothing.'

'You know, I'm very sure it does.'

She thought about it. He watched as she thought about it.

He saw more than she wanted him to see, she decided. His gaze was calm but intent, giving her all the time in the world to answer but getting answers of his own while he waited. She could see exactly what he was doing, but there was no escaping those calm, intelligent eyes.

'My chest,' she said at last, reluctantly.

'There's a bit of water in your lungs. We've X-rayed. It's nice clean ocean water and you're a healthy young woman. It shouldn't cause problems but we're giving you antibiotics in case, and you need to stay propped up on pillows and under observation until it clears. Your breathing's a bit ragged and it'll cause a bit of discomfort. We're starting you on diuretics—something to dry you out a bit. There'll be no long-term issues as long as you obey instructions.'

'My arms...'

'Harness,' he said ruefully. 'We try and pad 'em.'

'We?'

'New South Wales North Coast Flight-Aid.'

There was an echo—the way he said the name. Some time last night those words had been said—maybe even on the way up into the helicopter.

'*New South Wales North Coast Flight-Aid, ma'am, at your service.*'

Same voice. Same man?

'Were you the one who pulled me up?' she asked, astounded.

'I was,' he said, modestly. 'You were wet.'

'Wet?' She felt…disconcerted to say the least.

'Six years in med school,' he said proudly. 'Then four years of emergency medicine training, plus more training courses than you can imagine to get the rescue stuff right. Put it all together and I can definitely state that you were wet.' He took her wrist as he talked, feeling her pulse. Watching her intently. 'So, arms and chest are sore. Toes?'

'They're fine. Though I was a bit worried about them last night,' she admitted.

'You were very cold.' He turned his attention to the end of the bed, tugged up the coverlet from the bottom and exposed them. Her toes were painted pink, with silver stars. Her pre-bridal gift from one of her bridesmaids.

Not the bridesmaid she'd caught with Roger. One of the other five.

'Wiggle 'em,' Riley said, and she hauled her

thoughts back to toes. She'd much rather think of toes than Roger. Or bridesmaids.

So she wiggled then and she admired them wiggling. Last night she'd decided sharks had taken them, and she hadn't much cared.

Today... 'Boy, am I pleased to see you guys again,' she confessed.

'And I bet they're pleased to see you. Don't take them night-time swimming again. Ever. Can I hear your chest?'

'Yes, Doctor,' she said, deciding submission was a good way to go. She pushed herself up on her pillows—or she tried. Her body was amazingly heavy.

She got about six inches up and Riley was right by her, supporting her, adjusting the pillows behind her.

He felt...

Well, that was an inappropriate thing to think. He didn't feel anything. He was a doctor.

But, doctor or not, he was very male, and very close. And still gorgeous. He was...mid-thirties? Hard to be sure. He was a bit weathered. He hadn't spent his life behind a desk.

He wouldn't have, she decided, if he was a rescue doctor.

If it wasn't for this man she'd be very, very dead.

What do you say to a man who saved your life?

'I need to thank you,' she said in a small voice, but he finished what he had to do before he replied.

'Cough,' he ordered.

She coughed.

'And again? Good,' he said at last, and she repeated her thank you.

'My pleasure,' he said, and she expected him to head for the door but instead he went back to his first position. Perched on the backward chair. Seemingly ready to chat.

'Aren't you needed somewhere else?' she asked, starting to feel uneasy.

'I'm always needed,' he said, with a mock modesty that had her wanting to smile. 'Dr Indispensable.'

'So you save maidens all night and save everyone else during the day.'

'I'm not normally a duty doctor but we're having staffing issues. Plus I haven't finished saving this maiden yet. You want to tell me why Roger and Mum told us you were suiciding?'

'I wasn't.'

'I get the feeling you weren't. Or at least that you changed your mind.'

'I got caught in an undertow,' she snapped, and then winced. She sagged back onto her pillows, feeling heavy and tired and very, very stupid. 'I'm sorry. I accept it looks like suicide, but I just went for a swim.'

'After dark, on an unpatrolled beach.'

'It wasn't completely dark. I'd been in a plane for twenty-four hours. The sea looked gorgeous, even if it was dusk. There were people everywhere, having picnics, playing cricket, splashing around in the shallows. It was lovely. I'm a strong swimmer and I swam and swam. It felt great, and I guess I let my thoughts drift. Then I realised the current had changed and I couldn't get back.'

'You must be a strong swimmer,' he said, 'to stay afloat for eight hours.'

'Is that how long I was there?'

'At least. We pulled you up at four-thirty. The sea wasn't exactly calm. I figure you must badly want to live.'

'I do,' she said, and she met his gaze, unflinching. It suddenly seemed incredibly important that his man believe her. 'I want to live more than anything in the world. You see, I don't have to marry Roger.'

Fifteen minutes later Riley headed back to Intensive Care to check on Olive Matchens and he found himself smiling. It was a good story, told with courage and humour.

It seemed Pippa had been engaged for years to her childhood sweetheart. Her fiancé was the son of Daddy's partner, financial whiz, almost part of the family. Only boring, boring, boring. But what could she do? She'd told him she'd marry him when she'd been seventeen. He'd been twenty and gorgeous and she had been smitten to the eyeballs. Then he was lovely and patient while she'd done her own thing. She'd even broken off the engagement for a while, gone out with other guys, but all the time Roger was waiting in the wings, constantly telling her he loved her. He was a nice guy. Daddy and Mummy thought he was wonderful. There was no one else. She'd turned thirty. She'd really like a family. Her voice had faltered a little when she said that, but then she'd gone back to feisty. Why not marry him?

Reason? Two days before the wedding she'd found him in bed with a bridesmaid.

Bomb blast didn't begin to describe the fallout from cancelling the wedding, she'd told him. She'd figured the best thing to do was escape, leave for her honeymoon alone.

She'd arrived in Australia, she'd walked into the luxury honeymoon suite Roger had booked, in one of Australian's most beautiful hotels, she'd looked out at the sea, and she'd thought she had her whole honeymoon ahead of her—and she didn't have to marry Roger.

Riley grinned as he headed for Intensive Care. If there was one thing Riley loved it was a happy ending.

He thought of what would have happened if they hadn't found her. She was alive because of his service. She was a woman who'd been given a second chance because of the skills his team offered.

And she'd use it, he thought, feeling exultant. Right now she was exhausted. She lay in bed, her face wan from strain and shock, her auburn curls matted from the seawater, her body battered and sore, and still he saw pure spirit.

It felt fantastic. Helping people survive, the adrenalin rush of search and rescue, this was *his* happy ending. Solitude and work and the satisfaction of making a difference.

Solitude…

The morning's satisfaction faded a little as the nuances of the word hit home. The fact that his solitude was about to take a hit.

His daughter would be here on Friday. Lucy.

What to do with a daughter he hardly knew? Whose existence had been kept from him because he was deemed inconsequential—not important in the moneyed world Lucy must have been raised in.

There was money in the background of the woman he'd just treated, he thought. He could hear it in Pippa's voice. English class and old money. The combination brought back enough memories to make him shudder.

But the way the woman he'd just left spoke shouldn't make him judge her. And why was he thinking of Pippa? He now needed to focus on Lucy.

His daughter.

She was probably just coming for a fleeting visit, he decided. Her email had been curt to say the least. Flight details—arrival at Sydney airport Friday morning. An almost flippant line at the end—'If it's a bother don't worry, I'll manage.'

If it's a bother… To have a daughter.

Family.

He didn't do family. He never had.

He didn't know how.

But he could give her a place to stay. That had to be a start. He lived in a huge old house right by the hospital. Once upon a time the house had been nurses' quarters, but nurses no longer lived on site. Big and rambling and right by the sea, it was comfortable and close and why would he want to live anywhere else?

Last year the hospital had offered to sell it to him. For a while he'd thought about it—but owning a house… That meant putting down roots and the idea made him nervous. He was fine as he was.

He could see the sea when he woke up. He had a job he loved, surf at his back door, a hospital housekeeper making sure the rest of the house didn't fall apart… He had the perfect life.

His daughter wasn't part of it. She was an eighteen-year-old he'd never met—a kid on an ad-venture to Australia, meeting a father she didn't know. Had she always known who he was? Why had she searched for him? Had she been defying Mummy?

And at the thought of her mother he felt anger almost overwhelm him. To not tell him that they'd had a child…

Anger was not useful. Put it aside, he told him-self. He'd meet Lucy and see if she wanted him to be a part of her life, no matter how tiny.

She'd probably only stay a day or two. That thought made him feel more empty than before he'd known of her existence. It was like a tiny piece of family was being offered, but he already knew it'd be snatched away again.

Story of his life.

He shook his head, managed a mocking smile and shook off his dumb self-pity. Olive Matchens was waiting. Work was waiting.

He'd saved Phillippa Penelope Fotheringham. Pippa.

He did have the perfect, solitary life.

Once Riley left, an efficient little nurse called Jancey swept into Pippa's cubicle to tidy up the edges. Someone was collecting her toiletries from the hotel, she told Pippa, and she bounced off to set up a call to Pippa's mother. 'Dr Chase's instructions. He says if you don't talk to her she'll be on a plane before you know it.'

It was sensible advice. Jancey put the call through and Pippa managed to talk to her. Trying not to cough.

'I'm fine, Mum. I have a bit of water on my chest—that's why I sound breathless—but, honestly, there's nothing wrong with me apart from feeling stupid. The hospital's excellent. I'm only here for observation. I imagine I'll be out of here tomorrow.'

And then the hardest bit.

'No, I was not trying to kill myself. You need to believe that because it's true. I was just stupid. I was distracted and I was tired. I went swimming at dusk because the water looked lovely. I was caught in the undertow and swept out. That's all. I would never…'

Then…

'No, I don't wish to talk to Roger. I understand he's sorry, but there's nothing I can do about that. Tell him it's over, final, there's no way we're getting married. If Roger comes I won't see him. I'm sorry, Mum, but I need to go to sleep now. I'll ring you back tomorrow. You. Not Roger.'

Done. Jancey took back the phone and smiled down at her, sensing she'd just done something momentous. Pippa smiled back at the cheery little nurse and suddenly Jancey offered her a high-five. 'You go, girl,' she said, and grinned.

She managed a wobbly smile, high-fived in return and slipped back onto her pillows feeling… fantastic.

She slept again, and the nightmare of last night was replaced by Jancey's high-five—and by the smile of Dr Riley Chase.

Two lovely people in her bright new world.

Olive seemed stable. Riley was well overdue for a sleep but problems were everywhere.

School holidays. Accidents. Flu. It seemed half

the hospital staff was on leave or ill. And now they had a kid in labour. Amy. Sixteen years old. Alone.

She should not be here.

How could they send her away?'

'We need someone to stay with Amy,' Riley decreed. 'She's terrified.'

'I know.' Coral, the hospital's nurse administrator, was sounding harassed. 'But we can't special her. I have no midwives on duty. Rachel's on leave and I've just sent Maryanne home with a temp of thirty-nine. I know she shouldn't be alone but it was her choice to come here. She knows she should be in Sydney. Meanwhile, I'm doing the best I can. I've put her in with your patient, Pippa.'

Coral sounded as weary as Riley felt. 'That's why I could free up a nurse for Olive,' she said. 'I'm juggling too many balls here, Riley, so cut me some slack. Putting Amy in the labour ward now will scare her and she'll be alone most of the time. Putting her in with mums who already have their babies isn't going to work either. The obs cubicle is close to the nurses' station, and I'm hoping your lady will be nice to her. I've put them both on fifteen-minute obs and that's the best I can do. Meanwhile, we have Troy Haddon in Emergency—he's been playing with those Styrofoam balls you put in beanbags. He and his mate were squirting them out their noses to see who could make them go furthest, and one's gone up instead of out. Can you deal with it?'

'Sure,' Riley said, resigned. So much for sleep.

Pippa woke and someone was sobbing in the next bed. Really sobbing. Fear, loneliness and hopelessness were wrapped in the one heart-rending sound.

She turned, cautiously, to see. Right now caution seemed the way to go. The world still seemed vaguely dangerous.

When she'd gone to sleep the bed next to her had been empty. Now she had a neighbour.

The girl was young. Very young. Sixteen, maybe? She was so dark her eyes practically disappeared in her face. Her face was swollen; desperate. Terrified.

Last night's drama disappeared. Pippa was out of bed in an instant.

'Hey.' She touched the girl on the hand, and then on the face as she didn't react. 'What's wrong? Can I call the nurse for you?'

The girl turned to her with a look of such despair that Pippa's heart twisted.

'It hurts,' the girl whispered. 'Oh, it hurts. I want to go home.' She sobbed and rolled onto her back.

She was very pregnant.

Very pregnant.

As Pippa watched she saw the girl's belly tighten in a contraction. Instinctively she took the girl's hand and held, hard. The girl moaned, a long, low moan that contained despair as well as pain, and she clutched Pippa's hand like it was a lifeline.

Pippa hit the bell. This kid needed help. A midwife. A support team. She looked more closely at the girl's tear-drenched face and thought she was sixteen, seventeen at most.

She needed her mum.

The nurses' station seemed deserted. Pippa, however, knew the drill.

Hospital bells were designed to only ring once, and light a signal at the nurses' station, so pushing it again would achieve nothing. Unless…

She checked behind the bed, found the master switch, flicked it off and on again—and pushed the bell again.

Another satisfactory peal.

And another.

Three minutes later someone finally appeared. Dr Riley Chase. Looking harassed.

'She needs help,' Pippa said before Riley could get a word in, and Riley looked at the kid in the bed and looked at Pippa. Assessing them both before answering.

'You should be in bed.'

'She needs a midwife,' Pippa snapped. 'A support person. She shouldn't be alone.'

'I know.' He raked long fingers though his already rumpled hair, took a deep breath and focused. He glanced down the corridor as if he was hoping someone else would appear.

No one did.

He stepped into the cubicle.

Once again, as soon as he entered, she had the impression that he had all the time in the world. He'd crossed over from the outside world, and now he was totally in this one—only this time he was focused solely on the girl in labour.

The contraction was over. The girl was burrowed into the pillows, whimpering.

'Hey, Amy, I'm so sorry we've had to leave you alone,' he told her, touching her tear-drenched face with gentle fingers. 'It's hard to do this and it's even harder to do it alone. I did warn you. This is why I wanted you to stay in Sydney. But now you're here, we just have to get through it. And we will.'

Pippa backed away as he took both Amy's hands in his and held. It was like he was imparting strength—and Pippa remembered how he'd felt holding her last night and thought there was no one she'd rather have hold her. The guy exuded strength.

But maybe strength was the wrong word. Trust? More. It was a combination so powerful that she wasn't the least bit surprised that Amy stopped whimpering and met his gaze directly. Amy trusted him, she thought. For a teenager in such trouble...

'I want to go home,' Amy whimpered.

'I know you do. If I were you, I'd be on the first bus out of here,' Riley told her. 'But there's the little problem of your baby. He wants out.'

'It hurts. I want my mum.'

'I wish your mum could be here,' he said.

'Mum thought it was stupid to come.'

'So she did.' Riley's face set a little and Pippa guessed there'd been conflict. 'So now you're doing this on your own. But you can do it, Amy.'

'I can't.'

'Can I check and see how your baby's doing?'

Pippa didn't need prompting to leave them to it. She scooted back to her bed and Riley gave her a smile of thanks as he hauled the dividing curtain closed.

'You've been getting to know your neighbour,' he said to Amy. 'Have you two been introduced?'

Pippa was back in bed with the covers up, a curtain between them.

'No,' Amy whispered.

'Pippa, your neighbour is Amy. Amy, your neighbour is Pippa. Pippa went for a swim after dark last night and came close to being shark meat.'

'Why'd you go for a swim at dark?' Despite her pain, Amy's attention was caught—maybe that's what Riley intended.

'I was getting over guy problems,' Pippa confessed. She was speaking to a closed curtain, and it didn't seem to matter what she admitted now. And she might be able to help, she thought. If admitting stupidity could keep Amy's attention from fear, from loneliness, from pain, then pride was a small price to pay.

'You got guy problems?' Amy's voice was a bit muffled.

'I was about to be married. I caught him sleeping with one of my bridesmaids.'

'Yikes.' Amy was having a reasonable break from contractions now, settling as the pain eased and she wasn't alone any more. 'You clobber him?'

'I should have,' Pippa said. 'Instead I went swimming, got caught in the undertow and got saved by Dr Chase.'

'That's me,' Riley said modestly. 'Saving maidens is what I do. Amy, you're doing really well. You're almost four centimetres dilated, which means the baby's really pushing. I can give you something for the pain if you like…'

'I don't want injections.' It was a terrified gasp.

'Then you need to practise the breathing we taught you. Can you—?'

But he couldn't finish. Jancey's head appeared round the door, looking close to panic.

'Hubert Trotter's just come in,' she said. 'He's almost chopped his big toe off with an axe and he's bleeding like a stuck pig. Riley, you need to come.'

'Give me strength,' Riley said, and rose. 'Can you stay with Amy?'

'Dotty Simond's asthma…' she said.

Riley closed his eyes. The gesture was fleeting, though, and when he opened them again he looked calm and in control and like nothing was bothering him at all.

'Amy, I'll be back as soon as I can,' he said, but Amy was clutching his hand like a lifeline.

'No. Please.'

'Pippa's in the next bed,' he started. 'You're not by yourself.'

But suddenly Pippa wasn't in the next bed. Enough. She was out of bed, pushing the curtains apart and meeting Riley's gaze full on.

'Amy needs a midwife.'

'I know she does,' Riley said. 'We're short-staffed. There isn't one.'

'Then someone else.'

'Believe me, if I could then I'd find someone. I'd stay here myself. I can't.'

She believed him. She thought, fast.

This guy had saved her life. This hospital had been here for her. And more… Amy was a child.

'Then use me,' she said.

'You…'

'I know there's still water on my lungs,' she said. 'And I know I need to stay here until it clears. But my breathing's okay. I'm here for observation more than care, and if you can find me something more respectable than this appalling hospital gown, I'll sit by Amy until she needs to push. Then I'll call you.'

He looked at her like she'd grown two heads. 'There's no need—'

'Yes, there is,' Jancey said, looking panicked. 'Hubert needs help *now*.'

'We can't ask—'

'Then don't ask,' Pippa said. 'And don't worry. You can go back to your toes and asthma. I'll call for help when I need it, either for myself or for Amy. And I do know enough to call. I may be a twit when it comes to night swimming, but in my

other life I'm a qualified nurse. Good basic qualifications, plus theatre training, plus intensive care,
and guess what? Midwifery. You want to phone
my old hospital and check?'

She grabbed the clipboard and pen Jancey was
carrying and wrote the name of her hospital and
her boss's name. 'Hospitals work round the clock.
Checking my references is easy. Ring them fast, or
trust me to take care of Amy while you two save
the world. Or at least Hubert's toe. Off you go,
and Amy and I will get on with delivering Amy's
baby. We can do this, Amy. You and me…women
are awesome. Together there's nothing we can't
do.'

'You want me to ring and check she's who she
says she is?' Jancey asked, dubious. He and Jancey
needed to head in different directions, fast. Neither
of them liked leaving Pippa and Amy together.

'When you've got time.'

'I don't have time,' Jancey said. 'Do we trust
her?'

'She's a warm body and she's offered,' Riley
said. 'Do we have a choice?'

'Hey!' They were about to head around the bend
in the corridor but Pippa's voice made them turn.
She'd stepped out the door to call after them.

She looked…

Amazing, Riley thought, and, stressed or not, he almost smiled. She had brilliant red curls that hadn't seen a hairbrush since her big swim. She was slight—really slight—barely tall enough to reach his chin. Her pale skin had been made more pale by the night's horror. Her green eyes had been made even larger.

From the neck up she was eye-catchingly lovely. But from the neck down…

Her hospital gown was flopping loosely around her. She was clutching it behind. She had nothing else on.

'The deal is clothes,' she said with asperity. 'Bleeding to death takes precedence but next is my dignity. I need at least another gown so I can have one on backwards, one on forwards.'

Riley chuckled. It was the first time for twelve hours he'd felt like laughing and it felt great.

'Can you fix it?' he asked Jancey.

'Mrs Rogers in Surgical left her pink fluffy dressing gown behind when she went home this morning,' Jancey said, smiling herself. 'I don't think she'd mind…'

'Does it have buttons?' Pippa demanded.

'Yes,' Jancey said. 'And a bow at the neck. The bow glitters.'

'That'll cheer us up,' Pippa said. 'And heaven knows Amy and I both need it.'

Assisting at a birth settled her as nothing else could.

Amy needed someone she knew, a partner, a mother, a friend, but there seemed to be no one. Her labour was progressing slowly, and left to herself she would have given in to terror.

What sort of hospital was this that provided no support?

To be fair, though, Pippa decided as the afternoon wore on, most hospitals checked labouring mothers only every fifteen minutes or so, making sure things were progressing smoothly.

The mother's support person was supposed to provide company.

'So where's your family?' she asked. They were listening to music—some of Amy's favourites. Pippa had needed to do some seriously fast organisation there.

'Home,' Amy said unhelpfully. 'They made me come.'

'Who made you come?'

'Doc Riley. There's not a doctor at Dry Gum Creek, and they don't have babies there if Doc Riley can help it. Mostly the mums come here but Doc Riley said I needed…young mum stuff. So they took me to Sydney Central, only it was really scary. And lonely. I stayed a week and I'd had enough. There was no way I could get home but I knew Doc Riley was here so I got the bus. But the pains started just as I reached here. And I'm not going back to Sydney Central.'

That explained why Amy was in a relatively small hospital with seemingly not much obstetric support on hand, Pippa thought, deciding to be a little less judgmental about Amy being on her own.

'Why didn't your mum come with you?'

'Mum says it's stupid to come to hospital, but she didn't tell me it hurt like this. If you hadn't been here…' Another contraction hit and she clung to Pippa with a grip like a vice.

'I'm here,' Pippa told her as Amy rode out the contraction. 'Hold as tight as you need. Yesterday I was staring death in the face. It's kind of nice to be staring at birth.'

Riley was in the final stages of stitching Hubert Trotter's toe when Jancey stuck her head round the partition.

'She's good,' she said.

'Who's good?'

'Our night swimmer. She's been up to the kids'

ward in her gorgeous silver and pink dressing gown, and she did the best plea you ever heard. Told them all about Amy having a baby alone. Talk about pathos. She's borrowed Lacey Sutherland's spare MP3 player. She conned one of the mums into going home to get speakers. She's hooked up the internet in the nurses' station and she's downloaded stuff so she has Amy's favourite music playing right now. She also rang the local poster shop. I don't know what she promised them but the guys were here in minutes. Amy's now surrounded by posters of her favourite telly stars. Oh, and one of the mums donated a giraffe, almost as tall as Amy. Pippa has Amy so bemused she's almost forgotten she's in labour.'

'She's a patient herself,' Riley said, stunned.

'Try telling her that. Oh, and I managed to ring the number she gave us in England. I had a minute and I couldn't help myself—she had me fascinated. Her boss says send her back, *now*. Seems your Pippa left to get married two weeks ago and they miss her. Talk about glowing references. Can we keep her?'

'I'm not sure how we can.'

'Just don't give her clothes,' Jancey said, grinning. 'I'm off duty now. We're two nurses short for night shift but I've already stretched my shift to twelve hours. How long have you stretched yours?'

'Don't ask,' Riley said. 'Okay, Hubert, you're done. Pharmacy will give you something for the pain. Keep it dry, come back in tomorrow and I'll dress it again.'

'You'll be in tomorrow?' Hubert asked as Jancey disappeared.

'Maybe.'

'You're supposed to be the flying doc, not the base doc.'

'Yeah,' Riley said. 'Can you ring the union and let them know?'

'Riley?'

He sighed and straightened. 'That'd be me.'

'Amy's moving into second stage.' It was Mary, the night nurse who'd just started her shift. 'Pippa says you need to come straight away.'

She'd been having doubts about the ability of this small hospital to prepare adequately for a teenage birth, but the transition from the cubicle near the nurses' station to the labour ward was seamless.

A nurse and an orderly pushed Amy's bed into a labour room that was homey and comforting, but still had everything Pippa was accustomed to seeing. Riley was already waiting.

He smiled down at Amy, and Pippa was starting to know that smile. It said nothing was interfering with what he was doing right now, and his attention was all on Amy.

He hardly acknowledged her. She'd walked beside Amy's bed simply because Amy had still been clutching her hand. The moment Amy no longer needed her she should back away.

She was in a fully equipped labour ward. A doctor, a nurse, an orderly. She could leave now but Amy was still clinging. Her fear was palpable and at an unobtrusive signal from Riley it was the nurse and the orderly who slipped away.

What was going on?

'Hey, Ames, they tell me your baby's really close.' Riley took Amy's free hand—and Pippa thought if she was Amy she'd feel better right now.

But maybe that wasn't sensible. Maybe that was a dose of hormones caused by Riley's great smile.

'Don't tell me you're an obstetrician, too,' she said, and then she decided her voice sounded a bit sharp. That was uncalled for. She was, however, seriously thrown. Did this guy ever sleep? Hanging from ropes, rescuing stupid tourists in the middle of the night, sewing on toes. Delivering babies. But…

'Amy knows I'm not an obstetrician,' Riley said,

still talking to Amy. 'We have an obstetrician on standby. Dr Louise will be here in a heartbeat if we need her, but Amy has asked if I can deliver her baby.' He glanced at Pippa then, and his smile finally encompassed her. 'Amy has need of friends. It seems she's found you as well as me. I know it's unfair but are you okay to stay with us for a bit longer?'

'Of course I can. If I can sit down.'

His smile was a reward all on its own. There was also relief behind his smile, and she thought he'd be feeling the responsibility of being Amy's sole care person. Plus doctor.

'Okay, then, Amy,' he said, taking her hand just as a contraction started. 'You have me, you have Pippa and you have you. Pippa has her chair. We have our crib all ready. All we need now is one baby to make our team complete. So now you push. Pippa's your cheerleader and I'll stand around and catch.'

Then, as the next contraction swelled to its full power, he moved straight back into doctor mode. He was a friend on the surface but underneath he was pure doctor, Pippa thought as she coached Amy with her breathing.

And he was some doctor.

Amy was little more than a child herself. Her

pelvis seemed barely mature—if Pippa had to guess she'd have said the girl looked like she'd been badly malnourished. If this was Pippa's hospital back in the UK, Amy could well have been advised to have had her baby by Caesarean section.

'C-section's never been option,' Riley told her in an undertone as Amy gasped between contractions. How had he guessed what she was thinking? 'Neither is it going to be. Not if I can help it.'

'Why?'

'Amy comes from one of the most barren places in the country,' he told her. 'I persuaded her—against her mother's wishes—to come to the city this time. Next time she may well be on her own in the middle of nowhere. You want to add scar tissue to that mix?'

Amy was pushing away the gas and he took her hand again. 'Hey, Amy, you're brilliant, you're getting so much closer. Let Pippa hold the gas so you can try again. Three deep breaths, here we go. Up the hill, up, up, up, push for all you're worth, yes, fantastic, breathe out, down the other side. You've stretched a little more, a little more. Half a dozen more of those and I reckon this baby will be here.'

It wasn't quite half a dozen. Amy sobbed and swore and gripped and pushed and screamed…

Pippa held on, encouraging her any way she

could, and so did Riley. Two coaches, two life-lines for this slip of a kid with only them between herself and terror.

But finally she did it. Pippa was already emotional, and when finally Amy's tiny baby girl arrived into the outside world, as Pippa held Amy up so she could see her daughter's first breath, as Riley held her to show Amy she was perfect, Pippa discovered she was weeping.

Riley slipped the baby onto Amy's breast and Amy cradled her as if she was the most miraculous thing she'd ever seen. As, of course, she was.

The baby nuzzled, instinctively searching. Pippa guided her a little, helping just enough but not enough to intrude. The baby found what she was looking for and Amy looked down in incredulous wonder.

'I'm feeding her. I've had a baby.'

'You have a daughter,' Riley said, smiling and smiling, and Pippa glanced up at him and was astonished to see his eyes weren't exactly dry either.

Surely a rough Aussie search and rescue doctor…

Just concentrate on your own eyes, she told herself, and sniffed.

'She's beautiful,' she said, trying to keep her voice steady. She touched the baby's damp little head with wonder. No matter how many births she'd seen, this never stopped being a miracle. 'Have you thought about what you might call her?'

And Amy looked up at her as if she was a bit simple—as indeed she felt. Amy had just performed the most amazing, complex, difficult feat a human could ever perform—and Pippa had simply held her hand.

'I'm calling her Riley, of course,' Amy whispered, and smiled and smiled. 'Boy or girl, I decided it months ago. And I'm keeping her,' she said, a touch defiantly.

Riley smiled. 'Who's arguing? It'd take a team stronger than us to get Baby Riley away from her mum right now.'

'Have you been thinking of adoption?' Pippa said, because if indeed it was on the table it needed to be raised.

'Mum said I had to,' Amy said simply. 'But Doc Riley said it was up to me. He'll support me. Won't you, Doc?'

'It will be hard,' Riley said, gravely now. 'You know that.'

'I know,' Amy said. 'But me and this kid…after this, I can do anything. She's going to have all the stuff I didn't. She'll go to school and everything.' She peeped a smile up at Riley, her courage and strength returning in waves with the adrenalin of post-birth wonder. 'Maybe she'll even be a doc like you.'

'Why not?' Riley said. 'If that's what you both want, we'll make sure there are people who'll help you every step of the way.' He hesitated. 'But, Amy, Riley's best chance of getting that is if you don't have six more babies in the next six years.'

'You don't need to tell me that,' Amy said tartly, and she kissed her baby's head. 'No fear. I had this one because I was stupid. Me and her…we're not going to be stupid, ever again.'

Amy was wheeled away, up to Maternity to be in a ward with two other young mums. 'Because that's where you'll learn the most,' Riley told her. Pippa promised to visit her later, but Amy was too intent on her new little Riley to listen.

Pippa's legs were sagging. She sat, suddenly, and felt extraordinarily relieved the chair was under her. Even her chair felt wobbly.

Riley was beside her in an instant, hitting the buzzer. 'We need a trolley,' he told Mary when she appeared. 'Fast, Mary, or I'll have to pick her up and carry her.'

'In your dreams,' Pippa managed, with a pathetic attempt at dignity. 'No one carries me.'

'I believe I already have.'

'With the help of a helicopter.' She was trying to sound cheeky but she wasn't succeeding. In truth, the room was spinning.

'Warren's the only orderly,' Mary said. 'The trolley will be ten minutes. You want me to fetch a wheelchair?'

'It's okay,' Pippa said. 'I'll be right in a minute.'

'You'll be back in bed in a minute.' And to her astonishment Riley's eyes were gleaming with laughter and with challenge. 'Let's do without Warren or wheelchairs,' he said. 'Fancy inferring I'm inferior to our helicopter.' And before she could realise what he intended, he lifted her high into his arms.

She squeaked.

Mary giggled.

'He does weights,' Mary told Pippa, bemused. 'What you said…that's a red rag to a bull.'

'He's crazy.'

'He is at that,' Mary said, chuckling and holding the door wide to let Riley pass. 'You try getting workers' compensation after this, Doc Riley.'

'Workers' comp is for wimps.' Riley had her secure, solid against his chest, striding briskly along the corridor, past rooms full of patients and visitors, carrying her as if she was a featherweight and not a grown woman in trouble.

Trouble was right. If a doctor did this in her training hospital… To a nurse…

Worse. She was a patient. This was totally unprofessional.

She needed to struggle but she didn't have the energy. Or the will.

Trouble?

She was feeling like she really was in trouble. Like she wasn't exactly sure what was going on. He was making her feel…

'I should never have allowed you to help,' he muttered as he strode, his laughter giving way to concern. Maybe he was feeling just how weak she was.

She wasn't really this weak, she thought. Or maybe she was.

She thought about it, or she sort of thought about it. The feel of his arms holding her…the solid muscles of his chest…the sensation of being held… It was stopping lots of thoughts—and starting others that were entirely inappropriate.

This was why they'd invented trolleys, she thought, to stop nurses…to stop patients…to stop *her* being carried by someone like Riley. It was so inappropriate on so many levels. It made her feel…

'You're exhausted,' he said. 'It was totally un-professional of me to allow you to help.'

That shook her out of the very inappropriate route her thoughts were taking. Out of her exhaustion. Almost out of her disorientation.

'To allow Amy to have a support person?' she demanded, forcing her voice to be firm. 'What does that have to do with lack of professionalism?'

'You weren't her support person.'

'I was. If you hadn't allowed me to be, I would have discharged myself and come right back. Amy would have said "Yes, please," and it would have been exactly the same except that you wouldn't be carrying me back to bed.'

'In your extraordinary bathrobe,' he finished, and the laughter had returned. It felt good, she decided. To make this man laugh...

And there her thoughts went again, off on a weird and crazy tangent. She was totally disoriented by the feel of his body against hers. He turned into the next corridor, and the turning made her feel a bit dizzy and she clutched.

He swore. 'Of all the stupid...'

'It's not stupid,' she managed, steadying again. 'It's wonderful. Last night you saved my life. This afternoon we've helped Amy have her baby.

You've done a fantastic twenty-four hours' work, Dr Chase. Did I tell you I think you're wonderful?'

Mary bobbed up beside them, still chuckling.

'Don't tell him that,' she begged. 'Everyone does. It gives him the biggest head. Riley, really, are you about to hurt your back?'

'Nope,' Riley said. 'Didn't you hear what our patient said? I'm wonderful. Practically Superman. You can't hurt your back if you're Superman.'

'Superman or not, Coral says to tell you that you can't be a doctor in this hospital unless you get some sleep,' Mary retorted. 'Coral said you're to leave and go to bed. Now.'

'Immediately?'

'Put Pippa down first, but leave the tucking in to me,' Mary ordered, as they reached Pippa's bed. 'Off you go, Dr Superman. Sweet dreams.'

'I need to say thank you,' Pippa managed.

'So say thank you,' Mary said, sounding severe. 'Fast.'

Riley set Pippa down. He straightened and she felt a queer jolt of loss. To be held and then re-leased…

She was more exhausted than she'd thought. She wasn't making sense, even to herself.

Riley was smiling down at her, with that amazing, heart-stopping smile. A lifesaver of a smile.

'It's us who should thank you,' he said. 'You were great.'

Her pillows were wonderful. Life was wonderful. Riley was wonderful.

'You are Superman,' she whispered. 'You've saved my life—in more ways than one.'

'It's what I do,' Riley said. 'Superheroes R Us. Come on, Mary, let's see if we can find some tall buildings to leap.'

'You can leap all the tall buildings you want, as long as you do it off duty,' Mary said tartly.

'Goodnight, then, Pippa,' Riley said. 'We both know what to do.'

Sleep. It sounded good.

She slept, smiling.

She slept, thinking of Riley Chase.

A baby called Riley. A little girl…

Eighteen years ago his daughter had been born and he hadn't known. Marguerite had chosen to have her alone, or with her formidable parents, rather than let him into her life.

He'd thought he'd loved her. He'd thought she'd loved him.

He had no idea what love was. What family was.

He'd watched Pippa with Amy, and felt the strength between them, the instant bonding of two strong women. That was what he didn't get. Didn't trust. Bonding.

Family.

His daughter was coming. It was doing his head in; delivering Amy's baby, thinking back to how it could have been if he'd been deemed worth being a partner, a father. Family.

Yeah, like that was going to happen. He needed to sleep. Get his head under control.

Or surf. Better. No matter how tired he was, surf helped.

He strode out of the hospital, headed for the beach.

The thought of Pippa stayed with him. Pippa holding a baby girl.

Too much emotion. His head felt like it might implode.

When all else failed, surf.

CHAPTER THREE

SHE slept all night.

She was still right by the nurses' station. It was probably noisy, but there was no noise capable of stirring her.

When she woke, even the hospital breakfast tasted good. She must have been very close to the edge, she decided as she tucked into her leathery egg. She must have been very close indeed, if she was now appreciating hospital food.

Just the concept of food felt great. There'd be lunch in a few hours' time, she thought with a thrill of anticipation. Maybe there'd be a snack in between. Life stretched out before her, resplendent in its possibilities. She lay back on her pillows and thought: This is day two of my honeymoon, what's on today?

At around nine Jancey bounced in, accompanying an intern, and she was aware of a stab of disappointment. The young doctor was efficient, caring, thorough, all the things he needed to be—but he wasn't Riley.

'Dr Chase isn't usually in the wards,' Jancey told her as the intern moved off to sign her discharge papers. Pippa hadn't asked about Riley, but somehow Jancey sensed Pippa wanted to know. 'He's in charge of Search and Rescue, and he does clinics for our remote communities. That's enough to keep any doctor busy.'

'This is the base for Search and Rescue?'

'Yep. We have two crews, two planes and one chopper. There's some coastal work—stuff like rescuing you—but most of our work is clinics and patient retrieval from Outback settlements. It keeps us busy. It keeps Riley very busy.'

'So I won't see him again.'

'Probably not,' Jancey said, giving her a thoughtful glance. 'I know; it seems a shame. He's a bit hot, our Dr Riley.'

'That's not what I meant.'

'Of course it is,' Jancey retorted, grinning. 'I'm a happily married woman but it's still what I think. It's what every hot-blooded woman in this hospital thinks. He walks alone, though, our Dr Chase.'

'Like the Phantom?' Pippa queried, a bit nonplussed.

'In the comics?' Jancey smiled and nodded.

'Yeah, though doesn't Phantom have generations of Dianas, providing generations of little phantoms? As far as we know there's not a Diana in sight. Coral, our nurse-administrator, reckons he was crossed in love. Whoops,' she said as the baby-faced intern harrumphed with irritation from the corridor. 'I know, talking about Dr Chase's love life with patients is totally unprofessional but what's life without a bit of spice? And who's going to sack me with our staff shortage? Okay, I gotta go and minister to the sick, hold the hand of the learning. Will you be okay?'

'Yes.' How else was a woman to respond?

'Are you staying in town for a while?'

'The hotel's paid for until Sunday.'

'Then soak it up,' Jancey said. 'Sleep, spas, maybe a massage. But be careful. Our Dr Chase will be very annoyed if he has to rescue you again.'

'He won't do that,' Pippa assured her. 'It's taken a lot of trouble to finally be on my own. I'm on my lonesome honeymoon and it feels fantastic. I'm not about to need anyone.'

Some wonderful person had fetched her luggage from the hotel. Pippa dressed and said goodbye to the ward staff. Jancey offered to accompany her to the taxi rank, but first Pippa needed to see Amy.

Amy was in a ward with two other young mums, all getting to know their babies. A lactation consultant was working with her, and there were rumours that Riley Junior was about to have her first bath.

'You were fab,' Amy told her as she hugged her goodbye. 'You and Doc Riley. I wish I could have called her Pippa, too. Hey, maybe I can. Riley Pippa.'

'Don't get too carried away,' Pippa said, grinning. 'You're making friends all over the place. By the time you leave here, this young lady might have twelve names.'

'I won't be here long. I don't like being in hospital,' Amy confessed.

'You're not planning to run away?'

'I won't do that. I've promised Doc Riley I'll be sensible.'

'You and me both,' Pippa said.

It was great that she'd been able to help yesterday, she decided as she left Amy. It had made the terrors of the night before recede. It had made Roger's betrayal fade almost to insignificance.

Birth beat death any day, she decided—and it also beat marriage. Now to have her honeymoon…

Half an hour later the porter ushered her into her hotel suite and finally Pippa was alone.

Her honeymoon hotel was truly, madly scrumptious. It had been years since Pippa had spent any time in her parents' world and she'd almost forgotten what it was like. Or maybe hotels hadn't been this luxurious back then.

The bed was the size of a small swimming pool. How many pillows could a girl use? There must be a dozen, and walking forward she saw a 'pillow menu'. An invitation to add more.

Thick white carpet enveloped her toes. Two settees, gold brocade with feather cushions, looked squishy and fabulous. The television set looked more like a movie screen.

Two sets of French windows opened to a balcony that overlooked the sea. Below the balcony was a horizon pool, stretching to the beach beyond.

It was magnificent—but Pippa wasn't exactly into horizon pools. Or pillow menus.

She gazed around her, and the familiar feeling of distaste surfaced. More than distaste. Loneliness?

That's what these sorts of surroundings said to her.

She was an only child of wealthy parents. She'd been packed off to boarding school when she was six, but during vacations her parents had done 'the right thing'. Sort of.

They'd taken her to exotic locations and stayed in hotels like this. Her parents had booked her a separate room, not close enough to bother them. They had employed hotel babysitters from the time they arrived to the time they left.

As she got older she pleaded to be left at home. There she least she knew the staff—and, of course, there was Roger.

Roger was the only friend who was permitted to visit when her parents weren't around. He was the only kid who wasn't intimidated by her parents' wealth and ostentation. More than that, he'd been…kind. Three years older than she was, she'd thought he was her best friend.

But now…

She gazed at her surroundings—at a hotel room Roger had chosen—and once again she felt tired. Tired to the bone.

The intern had told her to take it easy. 'You've had a shock. Let your body sleep it off.'

Good advice. She looked down at her half-acre of bed and thought she'd come to the right place to sleep.

And to think?

She wandered out to the balcony and stared out to sea. This was why she'd swum so late on Sunday night—from here the beach practically called to her. A lone surfer, far out, was catching waves with skill.

She'd love to do that.

On the far side of the headland she could see the cream brick building of the North Coast Health Services Hospital. A busy, bustling hospital, perpetually understaffed. Perpetually doing good.

She'd love to do that, too.

And with that, the sudden thought—could she?

What was she thinking? Nursing? *Here?*

She was here on her honeymoon, not to find a job. But the thought was suddenly there and it wouldn't go away.

Nursing. Here.

Because of Riley?

No. That was stupid. Really stupid.

'You've been unengaged for less than a week,' she told herself. 'You nearly died. You've had a horrid experience and it's rattled you. Yes, you don't like fancy hotels but get over it. And don't think past tomorrow.'

But…to work in a hospital where she was desperately needed, to be part of a small team rather than one moveable staff member in a big, impersonal city hospital. To make a difference…

Would it be running away?

No. She'd run away to go nursing, deciding it was her career despite her family's appalled objections. Somehow this no longer seemed like running away.

Maybe it'd be finding her own place. Her own home.

'They won't take me till my lungs clear,' she said out loud, and surprised herself by where her thoughts were taking her.

Could she?

She needed to sleep. She needed to gain a bit of perspective. She'd been in the hospital for little more than a day: how could she possibly make a decision yet?

But she already had. Meanwhile… She eyed the ostentatious bed and managed a smile. 'Suffer,' she told herself. 'Unpack one of your gorgeous honeymoon nightgowns and hit that bed.'

Sensible advice. She was a sensible woman.

She did not do things on a whim.

Or not until tomorrow.

She hung a gold-plated 'Do Not Disturb' sign on her door and fell into bed. To her amazement she was asleep before…well, before she'd even had time to feel amazed.

She dreamed. Not nightmares, though.

Sensible or not, she dreamed of Riley.

He couldn't get her out of his head. Pippa.

Tuesday. Three days till his daughter came.

When he wasn't thinking about Pippa he was thinking about Lucy and the combination was enough to have him wide awake before dawn, staring sightlessly at the ceiling, trying not to think of anything and failing on both counts.

Tuesday. He and Harry had a short run this afternoon, collecting two patients and bringing them back for minor surgery tomorrow. He was due to take a remote clinic on Thursday at the settlement where Amy lived. If she was well enough they might be able to take her home. The rest of the week was quiet—except for emergencies.

He should think of Lucy's arrival. Plan. Plan what? It was enough to drive him crazy.

And on top of that...

Pippa.

He never should have carried her.

It had seemed right. No, he never carried patients unless in dire emergencies—he wasn't stupid—but with Pippa... To wait for a trolley when she was clearly dizzy, when she was wearing that ridiculous bathrobe, when she was clearly in trouble...

How many patients made him feel like Pippa did?

Maybe it was the voice, he thought harshly. Upper-crust English. Maybe that was his Achilles' heel.

Only it wasn't the voice.

He lay back on his pillows, allowing himself a moment's indulgence, letting himself remember the feel of the woman in the fluffy pink bathrobe.

A woman who smiled at Amy, who coached her, who cared. A woman who pushed herself past exhaustion because a sixteen-year-old kid needed her. Her skill had stunned him—she had been totally on Amy's side; she was a midwife any woman would love to have at a birth.

But he also saw her as…a drowning bride at the end of a rope over a dark ocean.

The vision wouldn't go away.

Phillippa Penelope Fotheringham.

Pippa.

Phillippa, he corrected himself harshly. English. Probably wealthy.

She was a nurse. Why would he think she was wealthy?

There was something about her…some intangible thing…the Roger story?

What did it have to do with him? Forget it, he told himself. Forget her. He did not need complications in his life. He already had a big one. Lucy

He glanced out the window. The sun was finally rising, its soft tangerine rays glimmering on the water.

Out at sea he'd have a chance to think. Or not to think.

Surf. And more surf. And medicine.

What was life other than those two things?

On Tuesday evening Riley went to see Amy. She was out on the hospital balcony, cuddling her baby and looking longingly at the sunset over the distant hills.

'Hi,' Riley said from the door, and she beamed a welcome.

'This is lovely,' she said. 'You're my second visitor tonight.'

'Second?'

'Pippa came back to see me, too. Look.' She held up a stuffed rabbit, small and floppy, with a lopsided grin that made Riley smile.

'Cute.'

How long ago had Pippa been in? How much had he missed her by?

These were hardly appropriate questions.

'You missed her by minutes,' Amy said, and he caught himself and turned his attention back to where it should be. To his patient.

'I came to see you.'

'Pippa asked if you'd been in.'

'Did she?' He couldn't help himself. 'Is she still staying at the same hotel?'

'She says her lowlife boyfriend's paid so she'll use it all. She's trying to figure if he has to pay the mini-bar bill. If he does then she's going to turn all those little bottles into a milkshake.'

He grinned. He could see her doing it. The girl had spunk.

More.

Pippa had been his patient. More was not appropriate.

'When can I go home?' Amy asked.

'I'd like you to stay for a week.'

'But you only go to Dry Gum every two weeks. You're due there on Thursday. If I don't go with you then I'm stuck here until next time.'

He hesitated. Four days post-delivery… He'd rather keep her here.

'I hate hospitals,' she said.

She didn't. It was just that she was lonely. And young.

Should he take her home? Medical needs versus emotional needs. It was always a juggling act. There was a medical clinic—of a sort—at Dry Gum. It wasn't perfect but he looked into Amy's anxious face and he thought it would have to do.

'If things are still looking good then we'll take

you,' he told her. 'But then I want you to stay with Sister Joyce for a week to make sure you know exactly how to care for your baby.'

'I know most of it,' she said. 'I practically brought Mum's kids up.'

She had, too. This kid had as much spunk as Pippa.

No. More. Pippa had clung to life for a night. Amy had been clinging to life for sixteen years. He'd known her since she was ten, a bossy little kid who ordered her tribe of brothers and sisters around, who herded them into clinic when she felt they needed it, who, he'd heard from others, had even been known to steal to get food for her siblings.

He'd felt sick when he'd learned she was pregnant. He felt like he'd personally failed her. Letting a sixteen-year-old kid get pregnant…

He couldn't protect them all.

He could try.

'There's still stuff you need to learn,' he told her.

'I know there is,' she said, serious in response. 'Sister Joyce'll teach me.'

'You will stay with Sister Joyce for a week?'

'Maybe longer,' she said diffidently. 'I'm not going home to Mum.'

That was a big step. Huge. Riley mentally rearranged his schedule and hauled up a chair. 'So Baby Riley's dad…' he said. As far as he knew this baby was the result of a relationship that had lasted less than a month. 'Jason?'

'He's gotta pull his socks up.'

'Yeah?'

'He wants to live with me,' Amy said. 'I asked Sister Joyce before I came here and she reckons she can get us one of the houses the government's built by the school. Wouldn't that be cool? I asked her if just me and the kid could go into it and she said yes. So I told Jason if he gets a job and sorts himself out he can come, too. Jason's okay.' She smiled then, a smile much wiser than her years. 'He'll be nice if I can keep him straight.'

If anyone could do it, it was Amy, Riley thought, in increased bemusement. Her look was suddenly fierce, determined, focused. 'You know, when you and Pippa were helping me, I thought… That's what I want to do,' she said. 'Be like Pippa. Sister Joyce'll help me. I'm can learn.'

'You're a lot like Pippa already,' Riley said, absurdly touched. 'You both have courage in spades.'

'Yeah, she's good,' Amy said. 'What a waste she has to go back to England.'

* * *

She didn't want to go back to England.

She was floating on her back in the sea. Of course she was going back. When you fall off a horse, get right back on. How many riding instructors had told her that?

It was Wednesday. The morning was gorgeous, the sea was glistening, there were flags showing the beach was patrolled and two burly lifesavers were watching her every move.

She wasn't stupid. She didn't go out of her depth. She just floated. Thinking...

What was there to go back to?

Her parents?

No. They wanted her to marry Roger. It had seemed such a neat solution, two sides of business meeting in marriage.

'Marry Roger now,' her father had said. 'You're wasting time messing about nursing. Get the family an heir.'

What sort of feudal system did he live in?

But Roger had been understanding for years, even when she'd said she wanted to break off their engagement and be free while she trained. He'd enjoyed himself then, too, she thought. They'd even discussed their respective boyfriends and girlfriends. Then, when he'd gently resumed pressure to marry, there had seemed no reason not to.

Looking back, she wondered… Had he been relieved to be given free time before he set about doing what he must to cement the family fortune?

It made her feel ill that she'd been so stupid.

'I just wanted him to be my friend,' she said out loud, and heard the neediness of the child within.

But she was no longer a child. She was in Australia. The sun was shining on her face. There were two bronzed surf lifesavers watching over her.

This place was magic, she thought. Whale Cove was two hours' drive north of Sydney. It was a town rather than a city, clustered between mountains and sea, and it had to be one of the most beautiful places in the world.

'But you can't stay in your honeymoon hotel for ever,' she told herself.

'Why not? Roger's paying.' She rolled lazily over in the shallows, thinking about the pros and cons of Roger. She'd made some enquiries before she'd come—enquiries that maybe she would have been wise to have made before she'd got so close to the wedding.

It seemed her bridesmaid hadn't been the only one. He'd gambled on her not finding out.

She had to face it—he'd wanted her money, not her.

Ugh.

Suddenly she found herself thinking of Riley instead, and it was a relief when his image super-imposed itself over her ex-fiancé's.

Riley gambled, too, she conceded. She remembered him holding her in that black-as-pitch sea.

You're safe. You don't need to hold on, I have you.

He gambled with his own life to save others.

Melodramatic?

No.

What was he doing now? Off saving more lives?

She rolled onto her back again, watching the lone surfer she'd seen before. He was seriously good.

The waves were forming far out, building and curving and finally breaking, twelve feet high or so at their peak, then falling away to nothing, running themselves out as the water became deep again. There must be a channel between those waves and the beach, because in close the water was calm. Where she was the surf built again to about eight inches. Just enough to float on. Up and down. Watching the surfer. Thinking of nothing.

The surfer caught a huge swell. He was sweeping in on its face then disappearing underneath as the wave curled.

She caught her breath. She'd seen this on videos; being in the green room, they called it, totally enclosed in a tube of water. She watched on, entranced, wondering where he was. Was he still upright?

The wave curled right over, smashing to nothing at the end where he'd entered, collapsing in on itself all the way along, slowly, slowly for its full length.

And out he came at the other end. Still upright.

Riley?

She was suddenly standing chest deep, her hands up to shield her eyes from the sun. Was she imagining things?

Maybe not.

It was time to get out. The sensation that Riley might be sharing her water-space was somehow disturbing. She caught the next tiny wave in, then wandered up to the lifesavers.

She motioned—casually, she hoped—toward the surfer.

'He's good.'

'He is,' the older lifesaver said. 'Bit driven, that one. Surfs no matter what the weather.'

'Who is he?' Though she already knew.

'That's our Doc Riley,' the other guy said. 'Puts himself out there, our doc. Great doc. Great surfer. Not bad with a billiard cue either.'

'Crap at darts, though,' the other guy retorted,

happy to chat on a quiet morning. 'The missus says I should let him win because he hauled her brother off his fishing boat when it went down. Doc'd hate that, though. Letting him win.' He gazed out at Riley who'd caught his next wave. 'I sometimes wish he'd come off out there and let someone else save him. Balance things up, like.'

'Like that's going to happen,' the other guy said, and then he turned back to Pippa. 'You're English. Tourist?'

'I'm here for my honeymoon,' she said. It felt absurd to say it. But good. Honeymoons were great if they didn't involve Roger.

'So where's the husband?'

'He never got past fiancé and I left him in England.' The casual conversation was starting to feel like fun. 'Isn't that the best place for fiancés?'

'If you say so.' The younger lifesaver was checking her out from the toes up, and she thought she deserved that. She'd practically thrown him a come-on line. 'Hey, he's coming out. Doc, I mean,' he said, motioning to the surf. 'That's early.'

And Riley was right...there. One minute Riley had been far out at sea, the next he'd surfed across the channel, caught one of the tiddler waves, then reached the beach before she'd figured whether she wanted to see him.

Why wouldn't she want to see him? She tried to think about it while he hauled his surfboard onto dry sand and strolled up to meet them.

The lifeguards greeted him like an old friend. She should greet him as well but she was too busy getting her breath back.

He looked… Awesome.

Weren't surfers supposed to wear wetsuits?

He was only in board shorts. He'd be a lot easier to handle in a wetsuit, she decided.

Handle?

Handle as in come to terms with. Handle as in greet like a casual acquaintance.

Not handle in any other way.

But the look of him… He was every inch a surfer, tall, tanned and ripped. He didn't look like a doctor. He looked like he should be…should be…

Maybe she should just stop thinking. Her silence was starting to be marked.

'Hi,' she managed at last, and he smiled, and that smile…. He had no right to look like that. It threw her right off balance.

'I thought it was you,' he said. 'Have you been looking after her?' he asked the lifeguards. 'This is Pippa, our floater from Sunday night.'

Whoa. How to embarrass a girl. But neither of

the lifeguards looked judgmental. Instead they looked impressed.

'You managed to stay out there for eight hours?'

'Not by choice.'

'I'd guess not,' the older lifesaver said. 'And not because of the fiancé left in England?'

'Um…no.'

'I thought you'd stick to the hotel pool,' Riley said, and then a mum yelled from the end of the beach that her kid had his toe stuck between two rocks and the lifeguards left them to go and see.

'More toe trouble?' Pippa said, striving for casual. 'You guys could start a collection.'

'We try to keep them attached,' Riley said. 'There's something a bit offputting about toes in specimen bottles. Even ones painted pink with stars. Are you okay?'

'I… Yes.' What else was a girl to say?

'Nightmares?' he asked, suddenly gentle. In doctor mode. Only he didn't look anything like any doctor she'd ever met. Standing in the sun with water dripping across his eyes, his wet hair sort of flopping, his chest glistening…

Do not go there.

'No,' she managed, and was absurdly pleased that she'd got the word out.

'How's the cough? Mary says you're booked at Outpatients this afternoon for a full check.'

'Cough's settled. I'm all better.'

'I'm pleased to hear it,' he said. 'How's the heart?'

She knew what he meant. Cardiovascular concerns didn't come into this. He was enquiring about Roger. 'Happy,' she said, a trifle defiantly.

'Sure?'

'I'm sure. I'm a bit humiliated but the honeymoon's helping. Especially as Roger's paying.'

'Good ole Roger. Bride living it up at his expense. Is he back at the coal face, paying for it?'

'Don't you dare feel sorry for him,' she snapped, and he grinned.

'I never would. I'm on your side.'

'Guys stick together.'

'Not me. I stick with my patients.'

'I'm not your patient,' she said, and he nodded, thoughtful.

'No. But you were.'

'Meaning you have to be loyal.'

'Meaning I can't ask you out to dinner.'

That was one to take her breath away. She fought for a little composure. It took a while. The way he was making her feel… Maybe it was a good thing she couldn't be asked out to dinner.

'So tell me about Amy,' she said, because he didn't seem to be making any move to leave, to walk away.

'Patient confidentiality.'

'You just told these guys I was the…what did you call me? Sunday night's floater?'

'That was a non-specific impression.'

'So give me a non-specific impression of Amy.'

He hesitated. He shaded his eyes and watched the surf for a bit and she wondered if he'd gone too far already. She was, after all, his patient.

But he didn't leave, and when he spoke his voice was low and lazy and she thought she was exaggerating her importance to him. He was simply settling into his morning on the beach and wouldn't be hurried.

'Amy's amazing,' he said at last. 'She deserves everything we can do for her and more. She's the oldest of ten kids and she cares for them all. She's bossy and smart and tough—she'll fight for what she needs and I've seen her bloodied by it. Only we let her down. We thought of her as a kid. The nursing sister out where she comes from at Dry Gum Creek was gutted when she found out she was pregnant. Her mother would never have told her the facts and Riley junior is the result.'

'So why is she here?'

'We can't deliver babies at Dry Gum—there's no resident doctor. Normally we bring the mums here two weeks before their babies are due but Louise, our obstetrician, was concerned at Amy's age. She thought she'd be better at the teen centre in Sydney. So we took her there but she ran away, here, where she knows me. Sensible or not, she trusts me and she made it here before the baby arrived. We can only be grateful she didn't hitch a ride all the way back to Dry Gum.'

'So now...'

'We'll probably take her home tomorrow.'

'There's no father?'

'That comes within patient confidentiality.'

'Of course.' She hesitated. 'Will you personally take her home?'

'That's what Flight-Aid does—when we're not pulling maidens out of the water after eight-hour swims.'

'I'm sorry,' she muttered.

'Don't mention it. If you know how good it felt to haul you up alive...'

'If you knew how good it felt to be pulled up alive.' She stared out to sea and thought of where she'd be if this man hadn't found her. She shuddered.

Riley's hand was suddenly on her shoulder, warm and strong and infinitely reassuring.

'Don't,' he said. 'Yes, we hauled you up, but you did most of it yourself. In a couple of hours you'd probably have drifted into the next bay and been washed up on the beach. You'd have faced a long hike home but you would have lived happily ever after.'

'We both know...'

'No one knows anything for sure,' he said. 'I could have been hit by lightning right now, while I was surfing. Do I have nightmares because I almost was?'

'There's not a cloud.'

'That's the scariest thing,' he said gravely. 'There's nothing else to pull lightning to except me. I feel all trembly thinking about how close a call I've just had.'

He looked...anything but trembly, she decided.

He also made her heart twist. There was enough gravity behind his laughter to make her think this guy really did care. He really did worry that she might have nightmares.

'There's a psychologist at the hospital,' Riley said gently, and she knew she was right. 'Peter's great with post traumatic stress. Make an appointment to see him. This week.'

She didn't need…

'Do it, Pippa,' he said. 'I should have made the appointment for you but it's…'

'Not your job?'

'I just scrape people off,' he said. 'It's other's work to dust them down. I was only in the ward on Monday because we're permanently short-staffed.'

'So now you're surfing.'

'Who's not on my side now?' he demanded, sounded wounded. 'Our team picked up two car-crash victims north of Dubbo in the wee hours. I'm off duty.'

'I'm sorry.'

'Don't be sorry,' he said, switching back to caring almost immediately. 'It doesn't suit you. You know…' He hesitated. Looked out to sea for a bit. Decided to say what he wanted to say. 'The world's your oyster,' he said at last. 'You're back in the water. You have a honeymoon suite in the most beautiful place in the world. I get the feeling you've been drifting. Maybe you could use this time to figure what you want. What's good for you.'

'Standing here's good.'

'It's a great spot to be,' he said softly. 'And the surf's waiting.'

Then, before she guessed what he intended, he

lifted his hand and brushed her cheek with his forefinger. It was a feather touch. It was a touch of caring, or maybe a salute of farewell—and why it had the power to send a shudder through the length of her body she had no idea.

She stepped back, startled, and his smile grew rueful.

'Pippa, I'm not a shark,' he said. 'I'm just me, the guy at the end of the rope. Just me saying goodbye, good luck, God speed.'

And with that he raised his hand in a gesture that seemed almost mocking—and turned and headed back to his surf, back to a life she had no part in.

If he'd stayed on the beach one moment longer he would have kissed her.

He'd wanted, quite desperately, to kiss her. She'd looked lost.

No matter how strong she'd been—walking away from the appalling Roger, managing not to drown, helping with Amy, all of those things required strength—he still had the impression she was flailing.

She was nothing to do with him. She was a woman he'd pulled out of the water.

Like Marguerite?

He'd met Marguerite on a beach in the South of

France. Of course. She had been there as it seemed she was always there, working on her tan. Wealthy, English, idle.

On a scholarship at university in London, he'd been on summer break, the first he'd ever had where he hadn't needed to work to pay for next term's living. His roommate had known someone who wouldn't mind putting them up. The South of France had sounded fantastic to a kid who'd once lived rough on the streets of Sydney.

He'd bumped into Marguerite on the second day in the water, literally bumped when she'd deliberately swum into his surfboard. She'd faked being hurt, and giggled when he'd carried her from the water. She'd watched him surf, admired, flirted, asked him where he came from, asked her to teach her to surf—and suddenly things had seemed serious. On her side as well as his.

The first time he met her parents he knew he was hopelessly out of his class, but he didn't care. For Marguerite didn't care either, openly scorning her parents' disapproval. For five weeks she lay in his arms, she held him and she told him he was her idea of heaven. For a boy who'd never been held the sensation was insidious in its sweetness. She melted against him, and the rest of the world disappeared.

Then reality. The end of summer. He returned to university and the relationship was over. For weeks he phoned her every day, but a maid always took his calls. Marguerite was 'unavailable'.

Finally her mother answered, annoyed his calls were interfering with her maid's work.

'You were my daughter's summer plaything,' she drawled. 'A surfer. Australian. Amusing. She has other things to focus on now.'

He thought she was lying, but when he insisted she finally put Marguerite on. Her mother was right. It was over.

'Oh, Riley, leave it. How boring. You were fun for summer, nothing more. You helped me drive Mummy and Daddy crazy, and it's worked. They still want to send me to finishing school. Can you imagine?' She chuckled then, but there was no warmth in her laughter. There was even a touch of cruelty. 'I do believe they're about to be even more annoyed with me, but they won't know until it's too late, and I'll enjoy that very much. So thank you and goodbye. But don't ring again, there's a lamb. It's over.'

She'd become pregnant to rebel? To prove some crazy point over her parents?

And Pippa?

Pippa was rebelling against her family as well—like Marguerite?

Don't judge a woman by Marguerite.

No, he told himself harshly. Don't judge at all and don't get close. He'd seen enough of his attempts at family, his attempts at love, to know it wasn't for him.

So why did he want to kiss Pippa?

He didn't. A man'd be a fool.

A man needed to surf instead, or find someone else to rescue.

Someone who wasn't Pippa.

She wandered back to the hotel, lay on the sun lounger on the balcony, and gazed out to sea.

Thinking.

'I get the feeling you've been drifting. Maybe you could use this time to figure what you want. What's good for you.'

And…

'We're permanently short-staffed.'

The idea of staying had taken seed and was growing.

To be part of a hospital community doing such good…

'It's romantic nonsense,' she told herself. 'Yes,

you should go back to nursing but you know your old hospital will give you your job back.'

But to live here…

She could make herself a permanent home. A home without the ties, the guilt, the associations of a family who disapproved of her, who'd never cease expecting her to be something she wasn't.

She could buy a house. Something small over-looking the sea.

Home. It was a concept so amazing she couldn't believe it had taken her until now to think of it. Maybe she'd never been in a place where the call had been this great until now. Like a siren song. Home.

She could put up wallpaper. Plant tomatoes. Do… whatever people did with homes.

Do it, she told herself. Now, before you change your mind.

And then she forced herself to repeat the question that had been hovering…well, maybe from the time she'd been hauled out of the sea.

Am I doing it because of Riley?

Don't be ridiculous. Her sensible self was ready with all the justification in the world. You're doing it because of you. It's time you settled, got yourself somewhere permanent. And Riley's hardly in the hospital.

He is sometimes.

There was a reason doctor/patient relationships were banned, she thought. Was she suffering a bad case of hero worship?

How could she be friends with Riley? The relationship would be skewed from the start.

'So what?' she muttered. 'I can avoid him. Is hero worship enough to stop me applying for a job, making a home in the best place in the world?'

Yes. Sleep a bit more. Think about it.

I can't drift, she told herself.

Give yourself another day.

Yes, but that's all, she decided. One more day of drifting and then...

Then move forward.

Toward Riley?

No, she told herself harshly. Toward a home. Nothing more.

CHAPTER FOUR

RILEY enjoyed Thursdays. He liked the flights to the Outback settlements. Today he was scheduled for a clinic at Dry Gum Creek and Dry Gum was one of his favourites. It was Amy's home. It was also the home of Sister Joyce, possibly the fiercest senior nurse in the state. He loved her to bits. He pushed open the door to the Flight-Aid office feeling good, and found Harry sitting at his desk, with news.

'No Cordelia,' he said morosely. 'Her head cold's worse and her German shepherd's in labour.'

They stared at each other, knowing each was thinking the same thing. Cordelia was a first-rate flight nurse but she was in her sixties, her health wasn't great and her dogs were growing more important than her work.

'We can go without her,' Harry ventured. Working without a third crew member was fine unless there needed to be an evacuation. There wasn't an evacuation due today—they were simply taking Amy home and doing a routine clinic.

But there was always a chance that a routine clinic would turn into an evacuation. Crews of two were dicey.

They had no choice.

'There's a note for you to go see Coral.' Harry said, shoving himself off the desk. 'Take-off in ten minutes?'

'I'll check what Coral wants first,' Riley said. Their nurse-administrator was good. She usually let them be—that she'd contacted them today meant trouble.

More trouble than a missing crew member?

'Are you sure?' Coral was short and almost as wide as she was tall. She was sitting on the far side of her desk, looking at Pippa's CV like it was gold. 'You really want to work here?'

'I'm not sure if I can get a work visa.'

'I'll have you a work visa in the time it takes my secretary to make you a coffee. You're a midwife?'

'Yes, but...'

'But don't say anything,' Coral begged. 'I'm reading this thinking I'm shutting up about two of your post-grad skills. I could have me a war if this gets out. The surgeons will want you. Intensive Care will want you. I want you. When would you like to start?'

'I need to find somewhere to live. I'd like to find a house but it might take time.'

'We have a house for med staff. Four bedrooms and a view to die for. You can move in this morning.'

'My hotel's paid until Sunday.'

Coral nodded, reflective. 'You are still getting over your ordeal,' she conceded. 'Riley'll say you should rest.'

'I'm rested.'

'Your chest okay?'

'I've been given the all-clear.'

'Hmm.' The middle-aged administrator gazed speculatively at Pippa. 'How about we break you in gently with a training day—give you an overview of what services we offer outside the hospital?'

'I'd love that.' She surely would. Her lone honeymoon wasn't all it was cracked up to be.

'Well,' Coral said, glancing with approval at Pippa's jeans and T-shirt, 'you're even dressed for it.'

'I'm not,' Pippa said, alarmed. 'I came with resort wear. I bought these jeans yesterday. I'll need to buy serviceable clothes if I'm to nurse here.'

'For where you're going, jeans are great,' Coral said, beaming. 'Just wait until I tell Riley.'

* * *

Coral's door was open. She was drinking coffee with someone. That someone had her back to the door but she turned as she heard him approach.

Pippa.

What was there in that to take a man's breath away? Nothing at all. She'd probably come here to thank them. Something formal.

She rose and she was wearing neat jeans and a T-shirt. She looked almost ordinary.

But this woman would never look ordinary. Yesterday on the beach in her bikini she'd looked extraordinary. Now, in jeans, she still looked...

'You two know each other,' Coral said, and he pulled himself together. Coral was intelligent and perceptive, and she was looking at him now with one of her brows hiked—like there were questions happening and she was gathering answers whether he liked it or not.

'I… Of course. You know Pippa's the one we pulled from the water? Who helped with Amy's baby?'

'I do know that,' Coral said, her brow still hiked. 'So you know she's skilled?'

'I know she's skilled.' He felt wary now and he wasn't sure why. Pippa's face wasn't giving anything away. If anything, she looked wary as well.

'I have Pippa's application to work for us on my

desk,' Coral said. 'Right here. It looks impressive. You've worked with her. Any reason I shouldn't sign her up on the spot?'

Pippa? Work here? There was a concept to think about. But Coral was giving him no time. Answer, he told himself. Now.

'There's no reason at all,' he said, and was aware of a stab of satisfaction as he heard himself say it. Was that dumb? No, because Pippa was an excellent nurse.

Yes, because the satisfaction he was feeling didn't have a thing to do with her competence. It was everything to do with her looking at him measuringly, those calm green eyes promising a man…

Promising him nothing. Get a grip.

'For how long?' he asked.

'Indefinitely,' Pippa told him. 'I don't want to go back to England.'

'You'll change your mind.'

It was Pippa's turn to hike an eyebrow. She had him disconcerted. Very disconcerted.

But he didn't have the time—or the inclination—to stand around being disconcerted. He remembered work with relief. Harry was waiting. Amy and her baby would be loaded and ready to go.

'This is great,' he said. 'Pippa, welcome to Whale

Cove Hospital. But can we talk about it later? I need to leave.'

'I've sent a message to the ward to hold onto Amy for fifteen minutes,' Coral said. 'We have a couple of things to discuss. First, I've told Pippa she can move into the medical house. You have four bedrooms. I assume there's no objection?'

They both stilled at that. He saw Pippa's face go blank and he thought he hadn't been part of that equation.

'You never said I'd be sharing with Riley,' she said.

'It's the hospital's house,' Coral said. 'Riley mostly has it to himself but we occasionally use it for transient staff.'

'I'm not transient,' Pippa said.

'I have a guest coming tomorrow,' Riley said over the top of her.

'You have four bedrooms.' Coral glanced at her watch, clearly impatient. 'If you have one guest, there are still two bedrooms spare. It should suit Pippa for the short term. I'm not going to knock back a great nurse for want of accommodation. Meanwhile, Pippa would like to work immediately but I don't want to put her on the wards until I'm sure she's fully recovered. Cordelia's not coming in. You need another team member. Pippa needs an overview of the service so I'm sending her out with you. Can you fit her up with a Flight-Aid shirt so she looks official? She can tag along while you can talk her through life here. You'll be back by late tonight. Pippa, I'll let you sleep in tomorrow—it'd be a shame to waste that honeymoon suite of yours. You can move into the house at the weekend, you can start here on Monday, and we can all live happily ever after. No objections? Great, let's go.'

It had happened so fast she felt breathless. She had a job.

She was flying over the Australian Outback in an official Flight-Aid plane. Harry was flying it. 'Dual qualifications,' he said smugly when she expressed surprise. 'Triple if you count me riding a Harley. Riley here doctors and surfs. He has two skills to my three. It's just lucky I'm modest.'

Harry made her smile.

The whole set-up made her smile.

The back of the plane was set up almost as an ambulance. Harry and Riley were up front. Pippa was in the back with her patients, Amy and baby Riley.

This was the start of her new life.

She was wearing a Flight-Aid shirt. The Flight-

Aid emblem was on her sleeve and there was a badge on her breast. She was about to attend a clinic in one of the most remote settlements in the world.

This time last week she'd been planning her wedding. Four days ago she'd been floating in the dark, expecting to die. Now she was employed as a nurse, heading to an Outback community to help Dr Riley Chase.

The man who'd saved her life.

He was a colleague. She had to remind herself of that, over and over. But in his Flight-Aid uniform he looked…he looked…

'Isn't Doc Riley fabulous?' Amy was headed home with her baby, and things were looking great in her world. She was bubbling with happiness. 'He's made me see so many things. You reckon one day my baby could be a doctor?'

'Why not?'

'I wish I'd gone to school,' Amy said wistfully. 'Mum never made me and there were always kids to look after. Then Doc Riley read the Riot Act and now they all go. My littlie'll go to school from day one.' She glanced at Amy's uniform. 'It'd be so cool to wear that.'

It did feel cool. Wearing this uniform…

Her parents would hate it, Pippa thought. They

hated her being a nurse, and for her to be a nurse here...

They still had Roger. They liked Roger.

They didn't like her.

She was getting morose. Luckily little Riley decided life had been quiet long enough and started to wail. That gave her something to do, a reason not to think of the difficulties back home. She changed the baby and settled her on Amy's breast. As she worked she marvelled at how neat everything was in the plane's compact cabin, how easily she could work here—and she also marvelled that she felt fine. She'd had a moment's qualm when she'd seen how small the plane was. If she was to be airsick...

No such problem. She grinned at mother and baby, feeling smug. Somehow she'd found herself a new life. She'd be good at this.

Flight-Aid nurse. Heir to the Fotheringham millions?

Never the twain shall meet.

'So do we use her straight away?'

Riley sighed. He was having trouble coming to terms with their new team player, and the fact that Harry was intent on talking about her wasn't helping.

'She doesn't have accreditation,' he said. 'She's an observer only.'

'But you've left her in the back with Amy.'

'Amy needs company and I'm feeling lousy company.'

'I can see that,' Harry said thoughtfully. 'So is it a problem that we're saddled with a young, attractive, competent nurse rather than our dog-smelling Cordelia?'

'Cordelia's competent,' he snapped.

'And Pippa's not?'

'We don't know that.'

'So you'd rather the devil you know.' Harry nodded. 'I can see that.'

No comment.

Riley was feeling incapable of comment. He sat and glowered and Harry had the sense to leave him alone.

So what was the problem?

The problem was that Riley didn't know what the problem was.

Pippa was a patient. He thought of her as a patient—only he didn't.

She had the same English accent as Marguerite.

He couldn't hold an accent over her.

No, but there were so many conflicting emotions.

Lucy was coming. His daughter. She'd have this accent as well.

His hands were hurting. He glanced down and realised he'd clenched his fingers into his palms, tighter than was wise. He needed to lighten up. Before Lucy arrived?

He hauled out his wallet and glanced at the picture Lucy had sent him when she'd contacted him three months ago. His daughter was beautiful. She was eighteen years old and she was so lovely she took his breath away.

He'd had nothing to do with her life. He'd been a father for a mere three months.

Even then…after that one email, sent from an address that had then been deleted, he'd flown to England and confronted Marguerite. Tracking her down had taken time but he'd found her, married to a financier, living in a mansion just off Sloane Square. She was still beautiful, taking supercilious to a new level, and bored by his anger.

'Yes, she is your daughter but purely by genes. She doesn't want you or need you in her life. If she contacted you it'll be because she's vaguely interested in past history, nothing more. I imagine that interest has now been sated. Why would she wish to see you? I don't wish to see you—I can't imagine why you've come. No, I'm not telling you where she is. Go away, Riley, you have no place in our lives.'

So tomorrow he was expecting a teenage daughter, coming to stay. And in the back of the plane was a woman called Pippa who was also coming to stay.

Two women. Identical accents.

Trouble.

'It must be bad, to look like that,' Harry said cheerfully, and Riley found his fists clenching again.

'Women,' he said. 'Maybe Cordelia's right. Maybe dogs are the way to go.'

'Women are more fun,' Harry said.

'You have to be kidding.'

For the last half-hour she'd been gazing down at a landscape so unfamiliar she might well be on a different planet. She was gazing at vast tracts of red, dusty desert, stunted trees growing along dry river beds, weird, wonderful rock formations, sunlight so intense it took her breath away, a barren yet beautiful landscape that went on for ever.

Dry Gum Creek was in the middle of…the Outback? There seemed no other way to describe it. Out back of where? Out back of the known world.

The little plane bumped to a halt. Riley hauled

open the passenger door and Pippa gazed around her in wonder.

Red dust. Gnarled trees and windswept buildings. Dogs barking at their little plane like it was an intruder that had to be seen off. A few buildings that looked like portable classrooms. A slightly more solid building with a sign saying 'General Store'. A big, old house that looked like it might have once been a stately homestead, but that time was long past. Corrugated-iron huts, scattered far out.

A couple of the rangy dogs came rushing to greet them. Harry fended them off while Riley swung himself up into the back to help Amy with the baby.

'Welcome to Dry Gum Creek,' Harry told Pippa. 'I hope you aren't expecting swimming pools, shopping malls, gourmet eating.'

She smiled, feeling pure excitement. 'I left my credit card at home.'

A couple of little girls were peering out from the hut nearest the plane. They were eleven or twelve years old, with skins as dark as Amy's.

'Did Amy come?' one of them yelled.

'She sure did,' Riley called. 'Come and meet your new niece.'

The girls came flying, all gangly arms and legs, looking as thrilled as if it was Christmas Day.

Riley handed Riley junior down to Pippa. 'Don't let the girls have her unless Amy says so,' he said in an undertone.

Amy was enveloped in hugs, and Pippa thought this was almost the reaction of kids welcoming their mother.

'She could just as well be their mother,' Riley told her, hauling equipment from the plane, and once again she was struck with this man's ability to read her thoughts. It was entirely disconcerting. 'They'd be lost without her.'

'Are you coming home?' one of the kids asked Amy. Amy shook her head. She disentangled herself from them a little and took her baby from Pippa.

'Nope. I gotta stay with Sister Joyce for a week. Then I'm gonna have one of the huts by the school. Me and Baby Riley will live there.'

'Will Jason live with you?'

'Dunno.' Pippa saw Amy's face tense. 'Where is he?'

'He's got a job,' the oldest girl said, sounding awed. 'He's out mustering cattle. He said to tell you.'

'Wow,' Amy breathed. 'Wow.'

'Mum says it's stupid,' the little girl said. 'She says he can live off the pension.'

'It's not stupid.' Amy looked back to Riley for reassurance and Riley was right beside her, his hand under her arm. Amy was sixteen years old. She'd given birth four days ago, and her confidence would be a fragile shell.

'We're taking Amy to Sister Joyce now,' Riley told the little girls. 'She'll stay there until she's strong enough to look after herself.'

'We'll look after her,' the oldest of the little girls said, and squared her shoulders. 'We're good at looking after people. Amy's taught us.'

'And Jason'll help,' Amy told her. 'I know he will. Like Doc Riley.' With Riley supporting her, her confidence came surging back and she peeped an impudent, teasing smile at Pippa. 'My Jason's got a job. How cool's that? My Jason's gorgeous. Even more gorgeous than Doc Riley. Though I bet you don't think so.'

What?

That was a weird statement, Pippa thought. Totally inappropriate.

So why was she trying really hard not to blush?

Pippa had been expecting a hospital but it wasn't a hospital at all. It seemed little more than a big, decrepit house with huge bedrooms. The woman in charge was an elderly, dour Scot with a voice like she was permanently attached to a megaphone. Sister Joyce. She introduced her to some of her residents while Riley started his clinic.

Harry, it seemed, was needed elsewhere. The water pump was playing up. While Harry was here, Joyce decreed, he might as well be useful, and Pippa got the feeling Joyce would be as bossy as she needed to get what she wanted for her residents.

Maybe she needed to be bossy. It seemed Joyce took care of sixteen patients on her own, and even though the place wasn't a hospital, the residents were certainly in need of care.

'We're not defined as a hospital,' Joyce told her. 'We're not even a nursing home because we can't meet the staffing ratio. A lot of our population is nomadic. Every time we try and take a census so I can get funding, everyone seems to go walkabout, so this is a sort of a boarding house with hospital facilities.'

'With you on duty all the time?'

Joyce gave a wintry smile. 'Don't look at me like that, girl. I'm no saint. This place suits me. I can't stand bureaucracy. I train our local girls to help me and I do very well. Amy's been the best. I have hopes she'll come back to work, baby or not. And we have Doc Riley. The man's a godsend. Sensible. Intelligent. He doesn't shove medical platitudes down people's throats. We've had medical professionals come out here with their lectures and charts of the five food groups, holding up pictures of lettuce. Lettuce! Our kids get two apples a day at school, they take home more, but even apples cost a fortune by the time we fly them in. Lettuce!' She snorted her disgust. 'You want to see what Riley's doing?'

'I… Yes, please.' They'd moved out on the veranda where half a dozen old men were sitting in the sun, gazing at the horizon. 'Are these guys patients?'

'Diabetics,' Joyce said. 'You look closely at their feet and you'll see. And half of them are blind. Diabetes is a curse out here. An appalling diet when they were young, a bit of alcohol thrown in for good measure, eye infections untreated, you name it. Most of these guys are in their fifties or sixties but they look much older. Riley's doing his best to see this doesn't happen to the next generation.'

He was. Joyce ushered her into a room at the end of the veranda. Riley was seated beside a desk. A dark, buxom woman who Joyce introduced as the local school teacher was shepherding a queue of kids past him.

'He's doing ear and eye checks,' Joyce told her. 'I do them but I miss things. There's seven steps to go through for each child to make sure they have healthy eyes. He also checks ears. These people are tough and self-sufficient—they have to be—but that causes problems, too. Many of these kids don't even tell their mums when their ears hurt. Infections go unnoticed. In this environment risks are everywhere. So we back each other up. Riley swears he won't let a kid go blind or deaf on his watch.'

'How long's he been doing this?'

'Six years now. He came to do an occasional clinic, then helped me set this place up. There was such a need.'

'How can you operate a hospital without a doctor?'

'We can't,' Joyce said bluntly, while they watched Riley joke with a smart-mouthed small boy. 'But we don't have a choice. We're three hundred miles from the next settlement and most of the older people won't go to the city for treatment even if it's the difference between life and death. I do what I can and Doc Riley is a plane ride away.'

'Always?'

'He's nearly as stupid as me,' Joyce said dryly.
'I need him, he comes. So... You're a qualified
nurse. English?'

'Yes.'

'I won't hold that against you. Coral said you're
here to watch. Sounds boring. Want to help?'

'Please.'

'You can speed things up,' Joyce said. 'Tell her,
Riley,' she said, raising her voice so Riley could
hear. He had a little girl on his knee, inspecting
her ear. 'I need to settle Amy in and help Harry
with the pump. Is it okay with you to let the girl
work?'

'Are you up to it?' Riley asked.

'You're not asking me to do brain surgery, right?'

He grinned. 'No brain surgery. We're doing ears
and eyes and hair and an overall check. You don't
know what you're letting yourself in for. Joyce and
I take every inch of help we can get.'

'I'd love to help,' Pippa said simply, and she
meant it.

So Riley kept on checking ears, checking eyes,
and Pippa took over the rest. She listened to small,
sturdy chests. She ran a quick hair check—it
seemed lice were endemic but she didn't find any.
She did a fast visual check of each child, checking

for things that might go unnoticed and blow up into something major.

The kids were good for Riley but they were like a line of spooked calves as they approached Pippa, ready for flight.

'Sam Kemenjarra, if you don't stand still for Nurse Pippa I'll tell her to put the stethoscope in the ice box before she puts it on your back,' Riley growled to one small boy. The little boy giggled and subsided and let himself be inspected.

But the line still fidgeted. Pippa was a stranger. These kids didn't like strangers—she could feel it.

'Nurse Pippa's been sick herself,' Riley said conversationally, to the room in general. He was looking at a small boy's eyes, taking all the time in the world. No matter how long the line was, she had the feeling this man never rushed. He might rush between patients but not with them. Every patient was special.

He was good, she thought. He was really good.

But then… 'She went swimming in the dark and nearly drowned,' Riley said. 'We had to pull her out of the water with a rope hanging from a helicopter.'

There was a collective gasp. Hey, Pippa thought, astonished. What about patient confidentiality?

But Riley wasn't thinking about patient confidentiality. He was intent on telling her story—or making her tell it.

'It was really scary, wasn't it, Pippa?'

'I… Yes,' she conceded. The line of children was suddenly silent, riveted.

'If I hadn't swung down on my rope to save you, what would have happened?'

She sighed. What price pride? Why not just go along with it? 'I would have drowned,' she conceded. So much for floating into the next bay…

'And that would have been terrible,' Riley said, and he wasn't speaking to her; he was speaking to the kids. 'Pippa was all alone in the dark. Floating and floating, all by herself, far, far from the land. There was no one to hear her calling for help. That's what happens when you go swimming in the dark, or even when it's nearly dark. Waterholes and rivers are really dangerous places after sunset.'

She got it. She was being used as a lesson. Her indignation faded. It seemed this was a great opportunity to give these kids a lesson.

It was also settling them.

'I thought something might eat my toes,' she conceded, figuring she might as well add corroborating colour. 'At night you can't see what's under the surface. All sorts of things feed in the water at night.'

'Crocodiles?' one little girl asked, breathless.

'You never know,' Riley told her. 'We don't have crocodiles here,' he told Pippa, 'so it's safe to swim in the waterholes during the day. But at night there's no saying what sneaks into the water looking for juicy little legs to snack on. And I wouldn't be here with my rope. It takes two hours for Harry and I to fly here.'

'But you'd come,' a little boy said, sounding defiant. 'If I went swimming at night you'd come with your rope.'

'It'd take me too long,' Riley said. 'Like Pippa, you'd be floating for a long, long time, getting more and more scared. You were really scared, weren't you, Pippa?'

'I was more scared than I've ever been in my life,' she conceded. 'I was all alone and I thought I was going to die. It was the scariest thing I can imagine. I know now. To swim at night is stupid.'

There was a moment's hesitation—a general hush while everyone thought about it. Then: 'I wouldn't do it,' the little boy declared. 'Only girls would be that stupid.'

'We would not,' the girl next to him declared,

and punched him, and the thing was settled. Night swimming was off the agenda.

'And while we're at it, we should warn Nurse Pippa about bunyips,' Riley said, still serious, and there was a moment's pause.

'Ooh, yes,' one little girl ventured, casting a cautious glance at Riley. A glance with just a trace of mischief. 'Bunyips are scary.'

'Bunyips?' Pippa said.

'They're really, really scary,' a little boy added. 'They're humongous. Bigger'n the helicopter.'

'And they have yellow eyes.'

'They sneak around corners.'

'They come up from holes in the ground.'

'They eat people.' It was practically a chorus as the whole line got into the act. 'Their teeth are bigger'n me.'

'You couldn't go night swimming here 'cos you'd get eaten by a bunyip first.'

'Or dragged down a hole for the little bunyips to eat,' the child on Riley's knee said, with ghoulish relish.

'You…you're kidding me,' Pippa said, blanching appropriately.

'Why, yes,' Riley said, grinning. 'Yes, we are.'

The whole room burst out laughing. Pippa got her colour back and giggled with them.

The room settled down to ears and eyes and hair and chests.

Pippa kept chuckling. She worked on beside Riley and it felt fantastic.

She was good. She was seriously good.

Cordelia was dour and taciturn. The kids respected her. They did what she asked but they were a bit frightened of her.

They weren't frightened of Pippa. They were enjoying her, showing off to her, waiting impatiently for Riley to finish with them so they could speed onto their check with Nurse Pippa.

Pippa. They liked the name. He heard the kids whisper it among themselves. Pippa, Pippa, Pippa. Nurse Pippa, who'd almost drowned.

He'd had no right to tell them the story of Pippa's near drowning, but the opportunity had been too great to resist. Drownings in the local waterhole were all too common, and nearly all of them happened after dusk. Kids getting into trouble, bigger kids not being able to see. Pippa's story had made them rethink. He'd told the story to fifteen or so kids, but it'd be spread throughout the community within the hour. Pippa's ordeal might well save lives.

And it had had another, unexpected advantage.

Somehow it had made Pippa seem one of them. She'd been given a story.

He'd brought many medics out here—there was genuine interest within the medical community—but mostly the visitors stood apart, watched, or if he asked them to help, the kids would shy away, frightened of strangers. But Pippa was now the nurse who Doc Riley had saved on a rope.

If Pippa was serious about staying...

She wouldn't be. She'd stay until she either made it up with her fiancé or she had her pride together enough to go home. It wasn't worth thinking of her long term.

But even if she was only here for a month or two...she'd make a difference.

He watched her as he worked, as she worked, and he was impressed. She was settled into a routine now, tugging up T-shirts, listening to chests, tickling under arms as she finished so the kids were giggling, and the kids waiting in line were waiting for their turn to giggle. She was running her hand through hair, saying, 'Ooh, I love these curls—you know, if you washed these with shampoo they'd shine and shine. Does Sister Joyce give you shampoo? See how my curls shine? Let's have a competition: next time I come let's see who has the shiniest curls. Every time you wash with shampoo they get shinier. No, Elizabeth, oil does not make curls shinier, it makes them slippery, and the dust sticks to it. Ugh.'

She had the capacity to glance at the child's medical file and take in what was important straight away.

'Can I see your toe? Doc Riley stitched it last month. Did he do a lovely neat job of it?'

Riley didn't have time to check the details Pippa was checking. Cordelia would have decreed it a waste of time. Cordelia followed orders.

Pippa was…great.

The day flew. He was having fun, he decided in some amazement. There was something about Pippa that lightened the room, that made the kids happy and jokey. Harry came in to check on their progress and stayed to watch and help a bit, just because it was a fun place to be.

How could one woman make such a difference?

Finally they were finished. They'd seen every school child, which was a miracle all by itself.

'Half an hour?' Harry said. 'That'll get us back to Whale Cove by dark.'

'I need to do a quick round of Joyce's old guys before I go,' Riley said. 'Plus I need to say goodbye to Amy. You want to come, Pippa?'

'Of course.'

'It's been a long day. I hadn't planned on you working.'

'I've had fun,' she said simply, and smiled, and he thought…

That maybe he needed to concentrate on the job at hand. He did *not* need to think of any woman like he was thinking of Pippa.

Why not?

The question had him unsettled.

Unlike Harry, who fell in love on average four times a year, he steered clear of even transitory commitment, but he did date women; he did enjoy their company. When he'd told Pippa on the beach that he'd like to invite her to dinner, it had been the truth.

But the more he got to know her the more he thought it'd be a mistake.

Why?

She was fascinating. She'd thrown herself into today with enthusiasm and passion. She'd made him laugh—she'd made the kids laugh. She loved what she was doing. She was…amazing.

And there was the problem. He looked at her and knew with Pippa he might be tempted to take things further.

He never had. Not since Marguerite. One appalling relationship when he'd been little more than a kid…

Except it was more than that. A shrink would have a field day with his dysfunctional family. He'd known three 'fathers', none of them his real one. He'd had stepbrothers and stepsisters, they'd always been moving home to escape debts, stupid stuff.

He'd escaped as best he could, physically at first, running away, sleeping rough. Then he got lucky, welfare had moved in and he got some decent foster-parents. There he learned an alternative escape—his brains. The library at school. A scholarship to study medicine, at Melbourne, then England. He'd earned the reputation of a loner and that was the way he liked it.

Only living at university he'd finally discovered the power of friendship. It had sucked him right in—and then he'd met Marguerite.

After Marguerite he'd tried to settle, only how did you learn to have a home? It didn't sit with him; it wasn't his thing.

When he'd come back from England he'd gone to see his foster-parents. They'd been the only real family he knew. They'd written to him while he was away.

They were caring for two new kids who were

taking all their energy. They were delighted that his studies were going well. They'd given him tea and listened to his news. His foster-mother had kissed him goodbye, his foster-father had shaken his hand, but they'd been distracted.

He wasn't their child. They'd done the best they could for him—it was time he moved on.

He did move on. His six years in Whale Cove was as long as he'd ever stayed anywhere. He took pleasure in the challenges the job threw at him, but still his restlessness remained.

He had no roots. A surfboard and enough clothes to fit in a bag—what more did a man need?

But as he walked along the veranda with Pippa, he thought, for the first time in years, a man could need something else.

But a man could be stupid for thinking it. Exposing himself yet again.

'Riley?'

Joyce's voice cut across his thoughts. That was good. His thoughts were complicated, and Pippa's body was brushing his. That was complicating them more.

'Yes?' His reply was brusque and Joyce frowned.

'Is there a problem?'

'Not with me there isn't,' he said, pulling himself up. 'I need to see Amy and then we'll go.'

'I'm sorry but I need you to wait,' Joyce told him. 'I've just got a message to say Gerry Onjingi's in trouble. They're bringing him in now. He was climbing the windmill at one of the bores and he fell off. They had pickets stacked up underneath. Gerry fell on one and it's gone right through his leg.'

They weren't going to leave before dark. Bundling Gerry into the plane and taking him back to the coast wasn't an option. Not with half a fence post in his leg.

For the men had brought Gerry in, picket attached. He lay in the back of an ancient truck and groaned, and Pippa looked at the length of rough timber slicing through his calf and thought she'd groan, too. Gerry was elderly, maybe in his seventies, though in this climate she was having trouble telling.

'Crikey!' Riley swung himself up into the tray the instant the truck stopped. 'You believe in making life exciting. This is like a nose bone, only different.'

'Funny, ha-ha,' Gerry muttered, and Riley knelt and put his hand on his shoulder.

'We'll get you out of pain in no time,' he told him. Joyce was already handing up his bag. 'Let's get some pain killers on board before we shift you inside.'

'Will I have to go to Sydney?'

And the way he said it… No matter how much pain he was in, Pippa realised, the thought of the city was worse.

'No promises, mate,' Riley said. 'We need to figure what the damage is. We'll get you out of pain and then we'll talk about it.'

It was amazing how such a diverse group of professionals could instantly make an elite surgical team.

Even Harry took part. By the time the morphine took effect, Harry had organised an electric buzz saw, with an extension cord running from the veranda. 'Electric's better,' he said briefly. 'Less pressure and this fitting's got fine teeth. It'll take seconds rather than minutes by hand.'

The picket had pierced one side of Gerry's calf and come out the other. Pippa helped Joyce cover Gerry with canvas to stop splinters flying. Riley and Pippa supported Gerry's leg while Harry neatly sliced the picket above and below.

'Closest I can get without doing more damage,' Harry muttered, and put the saw down and disappeared fast.

'Turns green, our Harry,' Riley said, grinning at

his departing friend. 'Still, if you asked me to pilot a chopper in weather Harry's faced, I'd turn green too.' He was slicing away the remains of Gerry's pants, assessing the wound underneath. It looked less appalling now there was less wood, but it still looked dreadful. 'Pippa, what's your experience in getting bits of wood out of legs?'

'I've done shifts in City Emergency. We coped with a chair leg once.' She made her voice neutral and businesslike, guessing what Gerry needed was reassurance that this was almost normal. Riley's question had been matter-of-fact, like bits of wood in legs were so common they were nothing to worry about.

'You got it out?'

'We did. When he came out of the anaesthetic the publican was there, demanding he pay for the chair.'

'So this little picket…'

'Piece of cake,' she said, smiling down at Gerry. Thinking it wasn't. The wood had splintered. The wound looked messy and how did they know what had been hit and not hit?

'Then let's organise X-rays,' Riley said. 'And an ultrasound.'

'You can do an ultrasound here?'

'Portable kit,' Riley said, sounding smug. 'Eat

your heart out, Sydney. Okay, Gerry, let's get you inside. Boys, slide that stretcher in beside him. Pippa, shoulders, Joyce hips, I've got the legs. And picket. Count of three. One, two, three…'

They moved him almost seamlessly and in less than a minute Gerry was in what looked to Pippa to be a perfect miniature theatre.

'I thought this place wasn't a real hospital?' she said, astounded.

'It's not.' Riley was manoeuvring the X-ray equipment into place. 'Dry Gum's too small for much government funding. Joyce is funded for a remote medical clinic, nothing more, but we have lots more. This place is run on the smell of an oily rag. Joyce and I do a lot of begging.'

'And blackmail,' Joyce said. 'Any company who wants to mine out here, who makes money off these people's land, can expect a call from me.'

'Joyce even buys shares,' Riley said in admiration. 'She's been known to get up in shareholder meetings and yell.'

'She's a ripper,' Gerry said faintly. 'Hell, if she had some money…imagine what our Joyce could do.'

'She's doing a fantastic job anyway,' Riley said. 'Okay, Gerry, that leg's positioned, everyone else behind the screen. Let's take some pictures.'

The leg wasn't broken. There was a communal sigh of relief.

The wood had splintered. Surgery would be messy.

The ultrasound came next and Pippa watched in awe. Reading an X-ray was one thing, but operating an ultrasound…

She could pick out a baby. Babies were big. Even then, when the radiographer said look at a close-up she was never sure she was looking at the right appendage.

But that Riley was competent was unquestionable. He was checking for damage that'd mean Gerry had to go to Sydney regardless. He was looking at flow in the main blood vessels—evidence that the artery was obstructed; blockage to blood supply that might turn to disaster when splinters were dislodged.

Despite the trauma Gerry seemed relaxed. As long as he didn't need to go to Sydney, whatever Doc Riley did was fine by him.

'I reckon we can do this,' Riley said at last. He cast a thoughtful look at Pippa. 'How tired are you?'

She was tired but she wasn't missing this for the world. 'Not tired at all,' she lied, and he grinned.

'Right. We have one doctor, two nurses and an

orderly. That's Harry. Green or not, he gets to keep the rest of the place running while we work. Pippa, you'll assist me. Joyce, are you happy to anaesthetise?'

'Sure,' Joyce said.

'You can anaesthetise?' Here was something else to astound. A nurse acting as anaesthetist…

'Joyce is a RAN, a remote area nurse,' Riley said. 'RANs are like gold. Sometimes she's forced to do things a doctor would blanch at, because there's no choice. We both do. Like now. I'm not a surgeon and Joyce isn't an anaesthetist but we save lives. If you end up working with us…'

'You'll get to do everything as well,' Joyce said briskly. 'Out here we do what comes next. Okay, Riley, let's not mess around. I have work to do after this, even if you don't.'

She had to ask. This was tricky surgery and to attempt it here… 'I know he's scared,' she ventured. 'But surely it'd be safer to take him to the city.'

'I can do it.' She and Riley were scrubbing fast, while Joyce was booming orders outside.

'Without a trained anaesthetist? To risk…?'

Riley paused then turned to her.

'Think about it,' he said harshly. 'Gerry's seventy years old and he's lived here all his life. No, that's not true. He's lived near here. For him Dry Gum is a big settlement. Even here is a bit scary. If I send him to Sydney I'll be throwing him into an environment that terrifies him. I'll do it if I have to, but it's a risk all by itself. I've had one of my old guys go into cardiac arrest in the plane and I'd swear it was from terror. With three of us… I've weighed the risks and they're far less if he stays here. Accept it or not,' he said grimly. 'We're doing it.'

By the time it was over Pippa had an even greater breadth of understanding of this man's skill. Quite simply, it took her breath away.

He took her breath away.

Joyce was competent but she wasn't trained in anaesthesia. That meant that Riley needed to keep an eye on what she was doing, checking monitors, assessing dosages, at the same time as he was performing a complex piece of surgery that frankly she thought should have been done in Sydney. By surgeons who'd had experience in such trauma, who had skilled back-up…

She was the back-up. She worked with an intensity she'd seldom felt. She was Riley's spare pair of hands and he needed her, clamping, clearing blood, holding flesh back while he eased, eased,

eased wood out of the wound. The splinters first of all and then the main shaft….

He had all the patience in the world.

It was a skill that awed her—this ability to block out the world and see only what was important right now.

Few people had it. A psychologist once told her it usually came from backgrounds where the skill was necessary to survive.

What was Riley's background? She didn't have a clue. All she knew was that there was no one she'd rather have in this room, right now, doing what he had to do in order to save Gerry's leg.

They worked on, mostly in silence except for Riley's clipped instructions. That fierce intensity left no room for theatre gossip, and she wouldn't have it any other way.

And finally, finally, Riley was stitching both entry and exit wounds closed. The stockman had been incredibly lucky. To have not severed an artery and bled to death in minutes… To have not even have fractured his leg…

'He'll stay with you for a week, though, Joyce,' Riley said in a seeming follow-on from Pippa's thoughts. 'There's a huge chance of infection. I'll put a brace on and tell him if it comes off in less than a week he'll have permanent nerve damage. It's a lie but it's justified. If he heads off back to camp, we'll have him dead of infection in days.'

'Won't antibiotics...?' Pippa started.

'He won't take them,' Riley said wearily. 'None of the older men will, unless we force-feed them. They see medicine as a sign of weakness. The women accept them now; they see how the kids respond and they believe. We're educating the kids, but Gerry missed out. So he'll wear an immobilising cast for a week. And I'm sorry, Pippa, but we need to stay here tonight until Gerry's fully recovered from the anaesthetic.'

She'd already figured that out. She'd been horrified that he'd attempt such surgery here, but having done it...he couldn't walk away with Gerry recovering from anaesthesia and no doctor on call.

'I can manage,' Joyce said, but Riley shook his head.

'I'll be the one who tells Gerry the rules in the morning. Can you put Pippa up here?'

'It's a full house,' Joyce said.

'Your sitting room?'

'Glenda Anorrjirri's in it,' Joyce said, apologetically. 'Her Luke's asthma's bad and she's frightened. They're staying with me until it's settled.'

'I told you—'

'To keep myself professional? I do,' Joyce said, flaring. 'I keep my bedroom to myself.'

'Which is a miracle all by itself,' Riley growled. 'Joyce has a one-bedroom apartment attached to the hospital,' he explained. 'She has a sitting room and a bedroom, which she's supposed to keep private.'

'I don't mind sharing with Pippa.'

'You're having your bedroom to yourself.' He was dressing Gerry's leg, and Pippa watched as he added a few artistic touches. Scaffolding from toe to thigh. A dressing around the lot.

'He'll think his leg's about to fall off,' Joyce said.

'That's what he's meant to think. You said you have a full house. Do you have room for him?'

'I was counting Gerry. He can have the last bed in Men's Room Two. But you and Pippa and Harry…'

'You know Harry sleeps on the plane. He doesn't trust the kids,' Riley explained to Pippa. 'Neither do I. Would you trust kids with a shiny aeroplane parked in their back yard?'

'You two could use Amy's place,' Joyce said, looking thoughtfully at Pippa. 'I have a little house ready for when she leaves here. There's a bed and a sofa in the living room. I know you have sleeping bags but I don't like the idea of Pippa sleeping rough.'

'I'm not nervous,' Pippa said, feeling nervous. 'I'm happy to sleep anywhere.'

'Pippa swims with sharks,' Riley said, and grinned.

He edged Joyce out of her position at the head of the table and started reversing the anaesthesia. 'Job well done, team. Thank you.'

'Nervous or not, you and Pippa will share Amy's house,' Joyce said.

Riley glanced at Pippa. His grin faded.

'I guess we will,' Riley said.

'Why not?' said Pippa.

CHAPTER FIVE

SLEEPING over was a common occurrence. Riley was used to it.

Harry slept in the plane. 'It's not half-bad,' he told Pippa. 'We have a comfy bed in the back and I always carry some fine emergency literature.' He grinned and hauled a fat paperback out of his back pocket. A buxom woman with tattoos, a dagger and not much else was pouting her lips provocatively on the cover. 'I'm happy as a pig in mud.'

Riley wasn't as happy.

They shared a late dinner with Joyce in the hospital kitchen, then it was time to head over to Amy's little house—with Pippa.

She seemed fine with it. He had the feeling she was even eyeing him askance because she was sensing he was edgy.

Why was he edgy?

Normally he'd roll his sleeping bag out and sleep under the stars. He'd lost count of the number of times he'd gone to sleep listening to Cordelia snoring, or medical students giggling, or sobbing and telling him their latest love life drama—sleeping under the stars did that for some. He didn't mind. He could listen to it all and keep his distance.

So tonight he'd much prefer to sleep under the stars, only that would leave Pippa in Amy's house alone. Or under the stars with him. And something told him…

Pippa wasn't as tough as she made out, he thought as they walked the short distance to the house. Five days ago she'd nearly drowned. He'd learned a lot about trauma in his years in this service— he'd had victims come back and talk to him about their experiences and he'd talked to psychologists. 'There'll be flashbacks,' he'd been told. 'You can't go so close to death without suffering.' And after eight hours in the water believing she'd drown… She'd been close to an appalling edge.

This trip had been meant to break Pippa in slowly, before sending her back to her luxury hotel tonight. To make her sleep outside… Personally he loved it but the sky was immense, and for someone already fragile… Someone who'd just re-entered the world of emergency medicine after being a casualty herself… Even Joyce had seemed to sense it.

It had to be Amy's house.

'I won't jump you,' Pippa said.

He stopped short. 'You won't…'

'I thought I should tell you,' she said. 'Joyce took me aside and told me you were honourable. You're looking worried. Maybe I should reassure you that I am, too. In fact I'm feeling exceedingly chaste. I guess that's what comes from being a jilted bride.'

'You don't sound very jilted,' he said cautiously. He was feeling cautious.

'I'm not,' she said. 'I'm exceedingly pleased to be free, so you needn't walk three yards away from me as if you're afraid I might latch on and not let go.'

'You're pleased to be free?' This conversation had him floundering.

'Yes, I am. I have the rest of my life ahead of me. I've had a very exciting afternoon and a very satisfactory day. I'm starting to make all sorts of plans but men aren't included. And I'm very tired. So show me a bed and then you can do what you want, but you don't need to look after me and you needn't think I'll be needy. I'm independent, Dr Chase, and I'm loving it.'

Only she wasn't.

He woke at three in the morning and she didn't sound independent at all.

Pippa was sleeping in the double bed in Amy's bedroom. Riley was on the fold-out settee in the living room.

It wasn't sobbing that woke him. It was gasps of fear, then the sounds of panting, breathless terror, muted as if the pillows themselves were drowning her.

If he wasn't a light sleeper he would have missed it, but Riley was a light sleeper at the best of times and he was awake and at her door before he thought about it.

Moonlight was flooding through the window.

Her bedding was everywhere. She was wearing panties and bra but nothing else. She looked like she was writhing in fear. Her curls were spread out on the pillows, and her eyes were wide and staring, as if she was seeing...

Hell?

It was enough to twist the heart.

'Pippa.' He was by her bed, grasping her shoulders, holding her. 'Pippa, wake up, you're having a nightmare. Pippa.'

Her eyes widened. She jerked sideways, as if he was the thing that terrified her.

'Pippa, it's Riley. Dr Chase. The guy in the helicopter. Pippa, it's Riley, the guy you're planning not to jump.'

And somehow the stupidity of that last statement got through. Her body stilled, slumped. Her eyes slowly lost their terror, and the terror was replaced by confusion. She focused. Her gaze found his. Locked.

She shuddered and the shudder ran the length of her body.

She was cold to touch. The temperature in the desert dropped at night to almost freezing. She'd gone to sleep with a pile of quilts, but the quilts were on the floor.

She shuddered again and it was too much. He tugged a quilt from the floor, wrapped it round her and tugged her into his arms. He held her as one might hold a terrified child.

She seemed so shocked she simply let it happen. The shudders went on, dreadful, born of fear and cold and sheer disorientation.

He should never have agreed to her coming here, he thought, swearing under his breath.

When he'd been a kid, tiny, he'd found a budgerigar—or rather one of the feral cats around the dump they'd been living in had found it. He'd managed to get it free, then brought it inside, warmed it and settled it into a box. A couple of hours later he'd checked and it had looked fine.

Delighted, he'd lifted it out. The little bird had

been someone's pet. It was tame, it talked, it clung to his finger, it pecked his ear.

With no adult to advise him, he'd played with it until bedtime. He'd popped it back into its box for the night and the next morning he'd opened the box to discover it was dead.

Years later he'd talked to a mate who was a vet, and he'd told him the sad little story.

'It'll still have been running on adrenalin,' the vet said. 'You weren't to know, but you'll have stressed it more.'

And today… He'd allowed Pippa to come here…

He'll have stressed her more.

He swore and held her close.

'It's okay, Pippa. You're safe. Yes, you're in the middle of the Australian desert with people you don't know, yes, you nearly drowned, yes, your marriage is off, but, hey, the threats are all past. No one and nothing's doing you harm. We'll get you warm, and tomorrow we'll fly you back to the coast. We're intending to fly via Sydney. You could catch a plane home to England from Sydney. How about if we phone your mother? That might make you feel like things are real.'

He was talking for the sake of talking, not waiting for a response, keeping his voice low and gentle, keeping the message simple. You're safe, there's no threat, you're under control.

The shudders were easing. She was curled against his body as if she was taking warmth from him, and maybe she was. He hadn't undressed to sleep—he'd hauled some rugs over himself and relaxed on the settee, knowing he'd be up two or three times in the night to check on Gerry. He was grateful for it now. He was in his Flight-Aid uniform. The shirt was thick, workmanlike cotton. If he'd undressed, as she had…

It'd be skin against skin…

And he could stop his thoughts going there right now.

He did stop his thoughts going there. Discipline. Nineteen years of discipline since…

'I'm…I'm sorry.' She was recovering enough to talk, but not enough to pull away. She was taking every shred of comfort she could find. Huddled against him, spooned against his body, wrapped in quilts, she needed it all. 'I shouldn't… I woke you…'

'Nightmares are the pits,' he said softly, and he smelled her hair and thought…and thought…

And didn't think. It was inappropriate to think. 'I didn't… I mean, I don't know why…'

'You didn't talk to the psychologists back at Whale Cove?'

'I didn't need to.' That was better. There was a touch of asperity in her voice. She had spirit, this woman.

If she didn't have such spirit she'd be dead, he thought, and the idea made him hold her tighter. For some reason…

Well, for a very good reason it was good she wasn't dead. But… Why was it *more* important that it was Pippa?

'I'm okay,' she said, but she didn't move.

'You're freezing. You pushed all the covers off. Stay where you are until you're warm.'

She was silent for a while and he could feel her gathering her thoughts, gathering her senses. Figuring out what had happened. How she'd ended up where she was.

'So I didn't have any blankets on?' she said at last, cautiously, and he grinned. The woman in her was back.

'Nope.'

'Oh, my…'

'Don't worry about it. I've seen worse things come out of cheese.'

She stiffened. She sat up and swivelled. 'Pardon?'

'I'm a doctor,' he said, apologetically. 'I learned anatomy in first year.'

'I am *not* your patient.' That was definite.

'No.'

'I'm your colleague.'

'Yes.' He thought about it. 'Yes, ma'am.'

He felt her smile rather than heard it and it felt good. To make her smile…

But suddenly he was thinking of her back in the water again, and this time it was he who shuddered.

'Hey,' she said.

'Sorry.'

'You're cold.'

'Nope.'

'I'm fine. You can go back to bed.'

'You're still shaking.'

'Not much.'

'I could go across and get some heat pads from Joyce.'

'No,' she said, and suddenly the fear was back in her voice. Born straight out neediness.

It had been some nightmare.

He'd had nightmares himself. As a kid. One of his stepfathers had enjoyed using a horsewhip. The beatings themselves hadn't been so bad. Waking up, though, in the night, when dreams blended reality into something worse…

Okay, he wouldn't leave her.

'The bed's big,' she whispered. 'Sh-share?'

He stiffened. She felt him stiffen, and he felt her immediate reaction. Indignation.

'We're colleagues,' she said, pulling away. Backing against the bedhead. Eying him with something that looked suspiciously like scorn. 'We have one bed. Why does everything have to be about sex?'

'I didn't think it was about sex.'

'It wasn't, until you reacted like that.'

'Like what?'

'Like I'd jumped you. Go back to your sofa.'

'No.' He could cope with her need, he thought. She was a colleague.

No. She was a patient. Think of her as a patient.

The lines were blurring. He wasn't sure how he thought of her. But he knew he couldn't leave her.

'Why not?' she demanded.

'Because one of two things will happen,' he said. 'Either you'll lie and stare at the ceiling for the rest of the night, scared to go back to sleep. Or you'll go back to sleep and the nightmare will be waiting. You're not out from it yet.'

'How do you know?'

He knew. If the shaking hadn't stopped…

'So what's happened to you?' she asked, her voice suddenly gentling, and that caught him so unawares he could have dropped her. Only he no longer had her. She'd slipped back onto the bed and only her feet were still touching him.

He wanted, quite badly, to be holding her again.

The thought jolted him. What was happening here?

He didn't react to women like this, but she'd somehow pierced something he'd hardly known he had. It was like she'd opened some part of him he'd been unaware existed.

It made him feel exposed. He had to get it sealed up again fast, but how could he do that while she was…here?

'Harry says you have a daughter.' Her voice was suddenly prosaic, like they were making polite conversation at a dinner party. She tugged her quilt. He let it go and she pulled it over her. She huddled under it and she tried to hide the next wave of shivers. 'What's her name?'

'Harry talks too much.' He sighed. 'Lucy.'

'You want to tell me about her?' She was eying him over the top of the quilt. 'I'm guessing Lucy isn't one of 2.4 children in a suburban back yard with Mummy in her apron and a casserole warming on the stove.'

'There are no slippers and pipe waiting at my place.' He said it almost self-mockingly and she slid to the far side of the bed and hauled one of her disarranged pillows to the empty side. She patted it.

'You want to tell me about it?'

She was still asking for help. He knew she was. She couldn't camouflage those tremors. This woman was needy.

So what was stopping him lying on the spare pillow, hauling up a quilt and telling her about Lucy?

Pride? Fear? Fear at letting someone as perceptive as she was close?

He wouldn't be letting her close. Or...no closer than she needed to be to get her warm.

She wanted distraction from terror. What harm?

He sighed. He slid onto the pillow and tugged up a quilt. Then, because it was what she needed and he knew it was, he slid an arm around her shoulders and tugged her close. She stiffened for a moment, but then he felt her relax. It was as if she, too, was reminding herself to be sensible.

'Back to front,' he growled. 'I can warm you more that way.'

'Wait,' she said, and sat up, grabbed her shirt and tugged it on.

Two Flight-Aid shirts. Colleagues.

'Needs must,' she said, lying down and turned her back, letting him tug her into him. He felt her force herself to relax. Muscle by muscle.

He was doing the same himself. The smell of her hair, soft and clean and with a scent so faint…if he wasn't this close he could never have smelled it.

'Tell me about Lucy,' she said, with sudden asperity, and he wondered if she realised what he was thinking.

If she had, then a man was wise to stop thinking it. Right now. Tell her about Lucy.

'She's my daughter.'

'I know that much.' She sounded amused.

'She's beautiful. She's dark and tall and slim. Maybe a bit too thin.' According to the one photograph he'd seen. What would he know?

'How often do you see her?'

'Never. I didn't know she existed until three months ago.'

'Wow!' She didn't sound judgmental. She just sounded…interested. It was the right reaction, he thought. She made it sound like not knowing you had a daughter was almost normal. That came from years of medical training, he thought. Nothing shocks.

'Wow's right.'

'Harry says she's coming tomorrow.'

'So it seems,' he said harshly. 'Let's talk of something else.'

'Something else.' She was silent for a while. Absorbing an absent daughter? He wondered if she was drifting into sleep, but apparently not.

'So what about your parents?' she asked.

'What about them?'

'Where are they?'

'My mother's in Perth. Last time I heard, my father was in New Zealand but that was twenty years back.'

'Not a close family, huh?'

'You could say that.' Family wasn't something he chose to talk about but if it stopped the trembling… This was therapy, he decided, and tugged her tighter and thought, Yep, medical necessity.

'You're so warm,' she murmured, and she was relaxing a little, warming a little, tension easing.

'So tell me about your family,' he said, deciding to turn the tables.

'What do you want to know?'

'Why your mother didn't get on that plane and come. She knew how close you'd come to death.'

'Just as long as it didn't hit the papers. That's all she'd care about.'

'Not close either?'

'Too close. They should have had more children. Only one…it's all your eggs in one basket and a girl can't live up to it.'

'Do they like you being a nurse?'

'They hate me being a nurse.' The tension was back again. 'I wanted to do medicine so badly but there was no way they'd support me. I was to go into the family business. That was my grandfather's decree. It's my grandfather who pulls the strings. I've had to work my way through nursing. He fought me every step of the way.'

'But you're doing something you love.'

'I'm not sure,' she whispered. 'Or…I am but I'm not doing enough. When I was trying to stop myself drowning, there was a part of me thinking… If I get out of here, I want to make a difference. Not just…be.'

'I can't imagine you just being,' he said, and she sighed and yawned and snuggled.

'It'd be so easy to sink into my parents' world. Like my hotel room. I have three different types of bath foam.'

'Really?'

'Really.' She snuggled again. His body was reacting. Of course his body was reacting. He'd have to be inhuman for it not to react.

He was wearing heavy-duty pants with a heavy-duty zipper. He was becoming exceedingly grateful that he didn't routinely pack pyjamas.

'I'm so warm,' she murmured. 'I shouldn't let you do this.'

'My pleasure.'

'I'm sure it's not.' Her voice was starting to slur. 'I'm sure it's just that you're a very nice man and a fine doctor. You saved my life and you've rescued me from my nightmare. Now you're making me feel wonderful. I'm so sorry you didn't know about your daughter.'

'I'm seeing her tomorrow. She's the guest I told Coral about.'

'That's great.' She sighed again, a long, sleepy, languorous sigh that made the night feel impossibly sensual. 'That's wonderful. Tomorrow you'll turn into a father. You're a lifesaver, a doctor, a father, a guy with pecs to die for…and you're holding me. Like three types of bath foam…what more could a girl desire?'

She was making no sense at all. 'Go to sleep.'

'I will.' She smiled—he heard her smile. 'I am. But I first I need to say thank you.'

'It's okay.'

'No, but tomorrow you'll be a father,' she said. 'And a doctor again, and a lifesaver, and I need to say thank you now.'

'Pippa...'

'You saved my life.' She was no longer even trying to make sense, he thought. She was simply saying what came into her head. 'You saved me from Roger. I could have married him.'

'That was hardly me...'

'You were part of it. If you hadn't been there for me... Apart from being dead...if it hadn't been you I might even have been weak enough to let him come. He might have bullied me into believing in him again. Marriage for the sake of family. Ugh.' She shuddered and clung.

'Not now, though. You've shown me how...ordinary it all was. Just ordinary.' Her voice was a husky whisper, part of the dreaming. Filled with pleasure and warmth and something more... 'Today... Not only am I alive, not only do I not have to marry Roger, there's a whole world you're showing me. You're showing me how it is to be alive. New. Wanting...'

'Pippa...'

Was she still dreaming? She wasn't, he knew she wasn't, but still she was in some dreamlike state where normal boundaries didn't apply. Saying exactly what she thought. Feeling what she wanted to feel. Loving the way she was feeling and letting him know that, too.

Her body was heating against his, and he knew… he knew…

That he should leave, now. Put her away from him. Let reality take over again.

But she was holding him, needing him, wanting him, and how strong would he have to be to put her away? She was a mature woman. She was melting against him, sensual, languorous, seductive…

Seductive?

'Thank you,' she murmured again, and before he could realise what she intended she twisted in his arms. She wound her arms around his neck, then pushed herself up, just a little, so she was gazing down at him in the moonlight.

And before he could even think how to stop her, or even if he wanted to stop her—she kissed him.

She surely kissed him.

For this was no kiss of thanks, a polite brushing of lips, fleeting contact and then pulling away.

This was a kiss of a woman wanting a man.

More.

It was the kiss of a woman claiming her man.

Her lips met his and the contact burned.

Maybe his whole body had been heating before

this point, and now… It was like the heat suddenly exploded into flame and the point of flame was his mouth, her lips, the melding of the two together.

This woman in his arms.

'Riley.' Had she said his name? She couldn't have, but the sound was between them, a long drawn-out sigh, a sigh of longing, of aching need, of want.

Of need between two people?

This was crazy. Unwise. Cruel even. To kiss her under such circumstances…

He wasn't kissing her—she was kissing him. But maybe the delineation was blurring.

Maybe they were simply kissing. A man and a woman and a need as primeval as time itself.

Pippa.

His defences were disappearing, crumpling at the touch of her loveliness, in the aching need of her sigh, in the heat of their bodies. He was kissing in return, demanding as well as giving, his mouth plundering, searching her sweetness, glorying in her need as well as his own.

Pippa.

She was like no woman he'd ever touched. His body was reacting without control. She was stripping him bare, exposing parts of him he never knew he had, parts hidden behind barriers he'd built up with years of careful self-restraint.

Where was the self-restraint now?

Certainly not with Pippa.

She needed this. He knew it at some basic gut level. She was a mature woman, a woman who knew her way in the world, a woman who fought for what she wanted. Or didn't want.

Right now she didn't want control.

Eight hours in the water had shown her, as his job showed him almost every day, that control was an illusion.

Pippa had cheated death. Her nightmares had brought it back but she was fighting past them.

Tonight was all about life, about affirmation of now. She was taking what she needed to survive.

This woman…

There were so many undercurrents, so many things he should make himself consider, but all he could think was how she felt in his arms. Her kiss, her mouth. Her hands holding him close, demanding he hold her close as well, growing closer… closer…

Her kiss was almost savage in its intensity—fire meeting fire. Sense was disappearing—had disappeared. There was only this woman.

There was only now.

Her fingers were unfastening the buttons of his shirt. He felt the tug, registered it for what it was, somehow made himself react. There was nothing between them but these clothes. If they disappeared...

He hauled back and it hurt, but he made himself put her away, holding her up from him, meeting her gaze in the moonlight.

'Pippa, if we go further...'

'Do you want to go further?' Her voice was steady, as it hadn't been steady until now. The tremors had ceased. She met his gaze squarely, surely, with honesty and with trust.

Trust. The sensation made something inside him wrench open. Barriers... Where were they? Not here. Not now.

'More than life itself,' he said, and knew it was true. 'But it's not wise.'

'I'm not feeling wise.' And before he could realise what she intended, she tugged her shirt off and tossed it aside. Her hands reached behind her back for her bra clip. 'Riley, I'm a mature woman. I've spent the night deep in horror. Yes, I'm using you. I know I am. Can you accept that? Want it even? I want it so much.'

He caught her hands and held. Stopping the bra disappearing.

'No.'

'No?' The tremor was suddenly back.

'Pippa, this is unprotected sex we're talking.'

'I'm supposed to be on my honeymoon. I'm protected.'

'You know as well as I do that—'

'That there's more risks than pregnancy?' Her eyes didn't leave his. 'There is that. I'm safe. Roger's a careful man. Double blind crossover tests, safe from everything except bridesmaids. How about you?'

'You shouldn't believe—'

'Neither should you. But I will believe. Can I be safe with you, Riley Chase?'

'You can be safe,' he said huskily, for the feel of her body over his was making his whole body seem to transmute into something he barely recognised. 'But, Pippa, is this purely to make you forget?'

'Forget?'

'Roger? Near drowning? Hopelessness?'

'No,' she said, surely and strongly. 'It's to make me remember. And before you ask,' she whispered, lowering herself again so her mouth was close to his, 'yes, it's seduction. Yes, I'm using you. I need you to affirm…life.'

She faltered then, suddenly unsure, but he knew it wasn't her actions she was questioning, it was her reasons. 'This night… You… It seems as natural as breathing. I've signed no contract yet at Whale Cove. Tomorrow I can walk away. I well may, because what happens tonight could make working together impossible. But it's not interfering with me wanting you now. And you…do you want me?'

How could she ask?

There was something changing within him. Something he hadn't been aware could be changed. The tenderness…the aching need he had for her…

Pippa.

Was she a fool?

She probably was, but she didn't care. She was in the middle of the Australian desert with a man she didn't know. Or maybe she did know him.

He'd saved her life but this went deeper. Something about Riley Chase resonated with her as no man ever had before.

Someday she'd ask him about his childhood, she thought. If she stayed around that long. If there was a shared tomorrow.

It didn't matter if there wasn't.

Or maybe it did matter, but for now she couldn't allow herself to care, for if she cared she'd allow in caution, rational thought, sense.

She didn't want those things. She only wanted Riley.

She'd told him it was to drive away nightmares. It was, but there was more. More she could hardly admit. More she didn't understand.

She was still resting lightly over him. She let her fingers run the length of his face, feeling the roughness of the stubble on his jaw, tracing the faint indentation of a scar at the side of his mouth, feeling the strength of his features.

She knew this man.

It was a strange sensation, but she believed it. She didn't need to know how he'd got that scar, where the life lines had been formed. Something within this man was stirring a response within her that she couldn't understand but could only believe.

Two halves of a whole? That was fantasy, but there was something. Some basic link.

If he told her now he'd had a happy childhood, a safe, secure existence, she'd never believe him. He was a man who walked alone. As she had, all her life.

As she would again tomorrow?

Maybe, but not tonight, for tonight she was holding Riley, and he was driving away every other thought. Taking away terror, giving her life.

She was exploring his face with her fingers,

loving what she was learning. She met his gaze, devouring the look of him.

There was need in his eyes. There was strength and truth and passion.

Another man might have taken what she offered without questions. He was still and silent, making sure…

He could be sure.

'Riley,' she whispered.

'Pippa.' He smiled at her.

And here was a wonder, for the smile said he was loving her. She knew it was just for now, but now was enough.

With his smile, the terrors of the last few days disappeared. As did the betrayal that was Roger, the accusations of her parents, the pressures from home. Even the awfulness of the sea; in the face of Riley's smile it was nothing. For now, for this wondrous moment, the horrors of the past made way. For Riley.

And then control was no longer hers. Impulse was no longer hers. For Riley took her face in his hands, he tugged her down to him, and he kissed her.

He kissed her as she ached to be kissed, a possessive, loving, searching kiss that said for tonight she was his woman and everything else must fade to nothing. This kiss was his seal of commitment. He deepened the kiss, and deepened it still more, and the sensation made her want to cry out with wonder.

He put her away from him once more and she almost cried a protest. But he was only moving her a little, so once more he could read her eyes.

'This is love-making,' he said softly. 'Pippa, what you're offering…it's a gift without price. I won't take it lightly.'

'I wouldn't expect you to,' she said, struggling to make her voice light in response. 'But I know it's only for tonight. You won't wake up to find your-self with a woman hanging on your sleeve, want-ing commitment. I've been engaged to Roger on and off for more than ten years. That's more than enough commitment. I've told my mother where she could put my wedding dress and it wasn't any-where polite.'

She smiled, finding shared laughter. Somehow she'd kept her voice steady. Somehow she'd made herself sound like she was telling the truth.

She didn't want commitment?

She was under control?

There was an illusion. The truth was that even though she was now independent, since last Sunday night her life had spun totally out of control, and Riley Chase was making it a thousand times worse. Oh, it was no fault of Riley's. She didn't even mind.

In truth, for the first time in her life she was out of control and she was loving it.

'So are you intending to kiss me again?' she teased. 'Because I'm getting a bit uncomfortable. I'm not sure if you've noticed but I'm lying on your chest and it's not quite as comfortable as that nice, soft mattress you're lying on.'

'Then let's fix that,' he growled, and swung her over so they lay side by side. And she was being kissed as she'd never been kissed in her life.

Riley was kissing her, tasting her, exploring her.

Riley was loving her.

And all that must be said had been said. Hesitations were gone.

She closed her eyes, savouring the feel of him, the taste, the touch. His hands were working their magic on her skin, knowing every inch of her, and every tiny movement sent shivers of sensual pleasure through her entire body.

She arched back and he found the clips of her bra. It finally fell away and she loved that it did. His fingers cupped the soft swell of her breasts, tracing her nipples, making her sigh with sheer, unmitigated pleasure.

She wanted closer. She had *his* buttons undone now—how had she done that? She hardly knew but his shirt was gone and she loved that it was gone. The feel of her skin against his…the strength of his body…the sheer maleness of him… It was taking her breath away.

The moonlight washed through the window, and the sight of his body was making her dizzy. His body heat, the touch of his mouth, the feel of his hands…

She was starting to burn.

His breathing was becoming ragged, and she gloried in it, gloried that he was feeling as she was. This was mutual need. Mutual pleasure. This was right, she thought, in some far recess of her mind. This man had given her her life, and this…it felt like giving life in return.

Her hair was tumbled on his face. He tucked her curls behind her ears and then tugged her tight so he could reclaim her mouth.

Oh, his mouth….

It wasn't enough. He was kissing her everywhere, a rain of kisses, her neck, her shoulders, her breasts, and the feeling was so breathtaking she could hardly take in air. Was that what was making her light-headed? She felt like she was floating, and he with her.

She was moving to another place. Moving to another life?

Her breasts were moulding to his chest as his hands tugged at her hips. Her clothing had disappeared entirely. Excellent, but fair was fair. She found the zipper of his jeans and tugged, and then her fingers returned to where the zip had been.

The night was swirling. Her mind was swirling.

Somehow she was shedding a skin, being hauled from her old life into this, the new.

Oh, the feel of him. The joy. He was discovering every secret of her body. She felt herself arch with sheer animal pleasure, abandoning herself to him entirely. He could do anything he wanted with her and she could do the same to him. For this night anything was possible.

The nightmares had faded to nothing. The terror that had lingered was gone, dissolved in Riley's heat, Riley's body, Riley's need.

Her need.

Skin against skin.

She couldn't get close enough.

She was on fire.

'Riley.' She heard herself moan but it wasn't her voice. It was a stranger, a woman Riley was loving. She heard the aching need and wondered at it. 'Riley.'

'My beautiful girl…'

And he was up and over her, his dark eyes gleaming in the moonlight. 'Are you indeed sure?'

Was she sure? For answer she reached and held his hips, she centred him, she tugged…

He was hers.

The night was dissolving around her. Riley…

'Pippa.' His voice was a husky whisper, in her ear. He was taking her slowly, with languorous pleasure, forcing her to wait, forcing himself to wait.

Riley.

This was where she was meant to be. This was her heart, her home, her centre.

This man.

He was a part of her, merged with her, one. Their bodies were riding each other, but there was no physical effort. Her mind was as clear as the stars outside. She came and came again but she didn't lose sight of Riley for one moment.

How could she close her eyes? She marvelled at his body as he moved within her. His raw strength. His muscles, delineated, beautiful.

Riley. For tonight, her man.

He was deep within her, and her body was taking her rhythm from his. He could take her anywhere he wished. He could love her for ever. This moment…

And the next.

For it went on and on, building, building, and she felt herself weeping with joy. She wept and she held his beautiful body and finally, wondrously, she felt him surge within her—and she knew nothing could ever be the same again. When finally he lay back, spent, when she lay on his chest and felt his heartbeat merged with hers, when she felt his fingers run through her hair with tenderness and wonder and love…

She knew the nightmares wouldn't return.

She knew he'd brought her out from the far side.

She just wasn't exactly sure he'd come out with her.

She slept, cradled in his arms, warm, secure, safe.

Pippa.

What had he done?

He'd slept with her.

He'd made love with her.

He'd never meant to. She'd been his patient. She was his colleague.

She'd woken in mid-nightmare. He'd come to comfort her and he'd taken her.

Or she'd taken him.

It was her need as well as his. What had happened had been the culmination of a need so basic it was almost past comprehension, past his ability to judge on right and wrong.

Because right now, lying in the dark with Pippa's naked body curled against him, it felt right. How could there be anything wrong with something that had felt so inevitable?

It didn't feel like he was holding Pippa. It felt like he was holding a part of himself. If something was to wrench her away right now, it'd hurt like tearing a part of himself away.

He turned his head a little and his face was in her hair. He was smelling the faint clean scent of her. She murmured a little in her sleep, her hand shifted, sought, held. His fingers were entwined in hers.

Pippa.

He was lying in the dark, holding his woman in his arms.

He closed his eyes and a peace he'd never felt before settled over him.

Right or wrong, for now, for this moment, Dr Riley Chase had come home.

CHAPTER SIX

SHE woke and he was gone.

She lay in the filtered dawn light and forced herself to absorb the fact without panic. She was trying to figure where she was, what had happened, what was real and what was dream.

She was naked. The bed smelled of love-making. There was a strong indentation in the pillow crushed beside hers. She rolled over and buried her face in the linen, thinking she could smell him.

She'd made love to Riley Chase.

She'd taken him…

She closed her eyes, letting the sensations of the night before unfold, reveal themselves, sort themselves into some sort of order.

She'd had a nightmare. Riley had come in to comfort her. She'd pulled him to her and she'd made love.

Talk about needy…

She should be mortified to her socks, only she

wasn't wearing socks. She was wearing nothing at all.

It felt excellent.

Her body felt new, like she'd done one of those crazy rebirth things she'd heard about. She smiled a little at that, thinking rebirth. Yes, she could have lain in a foetal position and pretended to be pushed, with a birth coach telling her exactly what to do. Or she could have taken Riley to her. She could have allowed him to take her. She could have woken feeling this…

Excellent.

Though maybe a bit sore. They'd woken during the night and made love again. And again.

She stirred and stretched and smiled. The tangerine of the desert sunrise was calling. Life was calling.

She flung off her bedclothes, headed for the shower, and went to find Riley.

Gerry had passed an excellent night. His leg was looking good and he wanted to leave, but the exceedingly large brace fastened from thigh to ankle was stopping him. Riley wasn't about to remove it any time soon. Gerry's wound was large and penetrating, there was access for infection everywhere, and he needed to stay right where he was.

'The nerves were millimetres away from being severed,' he told him. 'And you're not out of the woods yet.' No need to mention the two dangers were unrelated. 'I haven't saved your leg only to have you come back with gangrene or worse. You're staying in this bed for a week and we'll hear no more about it.'

He left the room grinning, and made his way to Amy's room. His grin faded.

Amy was cradling Baby Riley and she was crying.

'She won't feed,' she said. 'My boobs hurt, they're that full, but she won't feed. I fed her at midnight and she hardly drank anything and now she just wants to sleep.'

'Hi.' Pippa was suddenly in the room with them. She was a colleague, Riley told himself, trying hard to greet her as a colleague. But... How could she look so...neat? The last time he'd seen her...

Let's not go there.

'Problem?' Pippa asked, heading for the bed, professional even if he wasn't. Amy was cradling her baby against her breast. 'Hey, Baby Riley, who's a sweetheart?' She looked at Amy's swollen breasts, glanced at Amy's face, and Riley thought she had an instant appreciation of the situation.

'Who's a sleepyhead?' she asked. She stroked the

baby's cheek, the one closest to Amy's breast, and kept on stroking. The baby turned instinctively in the direction of the stroking. Pippa's fingers moved slightly, steering the baby's rosebud mouth. The little lips caught the taste of milk, caught Amy's nipple and started sucking. Though not with gusto.

'Keep stroking her cheek,' Pippa told her. 'No going to sleep, Baby Riley. You have growing to do.'

'She wouldn't…for me,' Amy said, choking back tears.

'I suspect she's a bit jaundiced,' Riley said, watching her suck. 'Not badly, but it's enough to make her sleepy.'

'What's jaundice?'

Pippa crossed to the basin and moistened a face-cloth. She washed Amy's face as Riley checked out his namesake. The baby was feeding but not with any energy. He checked her palms, then the soles of her tiny feet. Yesterday they'd been pink. Today there were faint traces of yellow.

Mild jaundice. Early days.

Watch and see, he thought. There wasn't any need for intervention yet.

But watch and see here?

'What's wrong?' Amy asked, breathless with

fear, and Riley uncurled the baby's fist and showed her.

'See her palm? The faint yellow tinge is the first sign of jaundice. It's common in babies. As our body's red blood cells outlive their purpose, our liver gets rid of them. If they can't, then we get a build-up of these old cells—the build-up's called bilirubin. Because Baby Riley's liver is so small, it's not doing its job properly. It might take a week or so to adjust.'

'But she'll be okay?'

'She'll definitely be okay. Sunlight helps. We'll pop her by the window with just a nappy on—that's often enough to fix it. The way you're feeding her now is great. It'll take a little more encouraging on your part and we need to make sure she's not getting dehydrated. If she gets any sleepier than she is, we'll pop her under lights like a sunlamp.'

'Sister Joyce will?'

'That's a problem,' Riley said evenly, as Pippa rinsed the facecloth and bathed her face again. 'Amy, jaundice usually shows up before this. If I'd thought Baby Riley might develop it, I'd have asked you to stay on in Whale Cove.' He met Amy's gaze square on. 'I'm sorry, Amy, but you need to come back with us.'

'To…to the hospital?'

'That would be best.'

'But I don't want to.' It was a wail.

'Then we can organise for you to stay in a hotel near the hospital. Amy, if you were living in Whale Cove I'd be saying keep doing what you're doing, give her a little sunbathe each day, call me if you need me. But I'm a long way away to call.'

Amy's bottom lip trembled. She really was very young, Riley thought. A child herself.

'Jason's out mustering,' she whispered. 'He's due back tomorrow. Can I wait until then?'

'I'm sorry. We need to leave this morning.'

'I don't want to go back to hospital. I hate hospital.' She was crying again, fat tears slipping down her face. She was afraid and alone, Riley thought, and he sent silent invective toward her mother. She hadn't even been in to see her daughter.

'Could one of your sisters come with you?' Pippa asked, diffidently, and he knew Pippa was thinking exactly what he was.

'Mum won't let 'em.'

'Could I talk to your mum?'

She would. He looked at Pippa, in her jeans and her Flight-Aid shirt, her hair bunched back into a loose braid, her face devoid of make-up, and he thought she was just as alone as Amy.

But she had courage in spades. Last night…she'd

known what she needed and she'd taken it. She'd taken *him*.

'She'd throw something at you,' Amy was saying, and Pippa blinked.

'Really?'

'Yeah. Or set the dogs on you.'

'Uh-oh,' Pippa said, and Riley smiled at her expression. A dog-setting, missile-throwing mother... Pippa had the sense to back away. 'Okay, that was option one,' she conceded. 'Option two is that you come back to Whale Cove and stay in the house beside the hospital where I'm staying. Where Doc Riley stays. They tell me it's okay to invite guests so I'm inviting you. Do you want to come and stay with me and Riley?'

She was... What the...?

Riley practically gaped.

'Close your mouth, Doctor,' Pippa said kindly. 'After all, it's not like Amy's a patient any more. This baby's called Riley Pippa, and that makes her our family. So will you come and stay with us?'

'But Jason...' Amy seemed bemused. She'd stopped crying.

'We'll leave him a note,' Pippa said grandly. 'If he can get to the coast then he can stay, too.'

'He probably won't want to.'

'That's up to him. Will you come and stay with us?'

'Yes,' Amy said, looking down at her drowsy baby, knowing she had no choice. 'Yes, I will.'

'Are you out of your mind?' Riley barely got the door shut behind them before he exploded. 'What sort of crazy idea is this?'

'What?' Pippa asked, turning to face him. She looked innocent and puzzled, as if she had no idea what he was talking about.

'Inviting Amy to live with me.'

'With us,' she said kindly. 'And not live. Stay.'

'You don't live in that house.'

'I do. Coral says I do. She says I'm to make it my home, so I am.'

'You're not due to move there until Sunday.'

'I'll need to move in straight away,' she said thoughtfully. 'That's a pity. Roger might even get a refund on his honeymoon suite.'

'She's a patient!'

'She's your patient. I met her in hospital when I was in the next bed. She's my friend.'

'You're a nurse.'

'Nurses have friends.'

'It's not ethical.'

'Why isn't it ethical?'

'You don't get involved.'

'*You* don't need to. Coral says you have a big bedroom and you barely use the rest of the house. I know your daughter's coming but Coral says we have four bedrooms. So how does having Amy staying get you involved?'

'You'll need to be involved.'

'I want to be involved.'

'Pippa...'

'Mmm?' She tilted her chin and met his gaze full on. Her eyes were direct and luminous.

He needed to keep building his anger, he thought. He needed to hold to his knowledge that she'd just overstepped professional boundaries, because suddenly all he could think of was how she'd felt last night.

How he'd held her.

How she'd slept, tucked into the curve of his body.

His boundaries were slipping. He felt them shift, and he didn't know what to do about it. Revert to anger?

'She'll have to go to hospital.'

'I've invited her to stay with us. She's stopped crying. You want me to go and tell her you've changed your mind?'

'I haven't changed my mind,' he said explosively. 'It's you…'

'Maybe you could stay in the honeymoon suite,' she said, thoughtfully. 'Though I'm not sure how I'd explain that to Roger. And then there's Lucy…'

'Of all the…'

'You don't want a honeymoon?'

'No! Neither do I want people staying in my house.'

'Coral said it's the hospital's house. And you already have Lucy.' She sighed, suddenly repentant. 'I'm sorry. I know I should have talked to you before I offered, but I couldn't bear it. She's so alone. I know what it's like to be alone, Riley, and I suspect you do, too, but I've never been as alone as Amy is right now. I can fix that. I'll take care of her.'

'You'll be working.'

'I will be,' she said, her tone suddenly severe as his objections grew weaker. 'You think Amy wants me there twenty-four seven? She'll take what I can give, but that's a whole lot more than she has now. So…are we heading back to Whale Cove or not?'

'Pippa…'

'Yes?' Her eyes were now expressionless. She was waiting for more anger, he thought. She was expecting more anger.

He didn't have it in him. Not when he looked at her.

'Last night...' he said.

'Was wonderful,' she said, quickly, before he could go any further. 'But you needn't worry. Yes, I used you to escape from my nightmares and, yes, it was fabulous, but I'm not about to step over the boundaries there either.'

'That's not what I was about to say.'

'Then what were you about to say?'

'That I thought it was wonderful, too,' he said, and her face lit in response, softening, her eyes lighting with laughter. She hadn't expected him to say it. She loved it that he had, he thought, and that felt...excellent.

'Snap,' she said, and she stood on tiptoe and kissed him, on the lips but lightly, fleetingly. 'It was indeed wonderful,' she said. 'But it doesn't mean I'm pushing past your boundaries. I needed you last night and you were there. I'll always be grateful. And now I intend to be there for Amy. See, we're both soft touches in our own way.'

'I didn't... Last night was more...'

'I know it was,' she said, firmly and surely. 'Like I said, it was fabulous. I'll remember it for ever. But we both know it was for one night only. We both know we need to love that it happened, and now we need to move on.'

They couldn't move on, not for a couple of hours. Joyce was waiting for them and cornered them before they reached the veranda.

'Ear infection,' she said. 'Coming in within half an hour. I'll make you breakfast. And while you're waiting, I'm concerned about John Thalderson's feet. He's cracked his heel,' she explained to Pippa. 'He's diabetic—lousy circulation. I'm dressing it every day but he came in ten minutes ago… Have a look, Riley, while I cook you breakfast.'

They both looked. John Thalderson's feet were truly appalling. He should be headed for Sydney, Pippa thought, or Whale Cove at the very least, but once again neither he nor Riley seemed to think it was an option.

Riley injected local so he could do a thorough debridement, cleaning up the messy edges. He dressed the wound with care, while Pippa assisted.

'You'll stay on the veranda for the week,' Riley told him. 'No argument. Look after Gerry for me.'

'Sure thing, Doc,' John said, and limped out, leaning heavily on his stick.

'Why not Whale Cove?' Pippa asked. 'He's not

about to go into cardiac arrest and surely he needs intensive, long-term treatment.'

'I told you,' Riley growled. 'I can't risk it. He'll lie in a clean white hospital bed, he won't eat the food, he'll turn his face to the wall and he'll get worse, not better. Yes, here his feet may well not heal. He may even face amputation, but even if he does we'll take him down to Whale Cove, we'll get it done as fast as we can and we'll get him back on this veranda. He'll certainly die faster than he would if he had optimum treatment but that's his choice.'

'So what Joyce is doing...'

'She's saving lives,' Riley said. 'By running this place and by turning her back on government regulations, she's keeping these guys alive, and I'm doing all in my power to help her. And now...she's even cooking bacon and eggs for us, so we're not keeping her waiting.'

Breakfast was massive.

Pippa ate and thought. Ate and watched. Then watched and listened, while hunger grew for something that had nothing to do with food.

Harry and Riley and Joyce chatted like the old friends they obviously were. They were doing such good, she thought. The three of them.

She wanted to be a part of it. Fiercely. More fiercely every moment.

Had she messed with that by sleeping with Riley?

Maybe she had. He was terse with her this morning, like he wasn't quite sure how to react. That was fair. She wasn't sure how to react to him either. And she'd foisted Amy onto him.

He was laughing at a story Joyce was telling him. The dour nurse thought the world of him. She could see it in the way Joyce smiled at him, the way she ladled more and more bacon onto his plate.

A team…

She wanted to be a part of it so much it hurt. She set down her knife and fork and pushed her plate away. Joyce looked at her in concern. 'Had enough?'

'I'm feeling disoriented,' she confessed. 'Like it's taking some time for my head to catch up with my body.'

'You're doing too much,' Riley said. 'We'll get you back to Whale Cove and you and Amy can lie on the veranda and let your heads catch up all they want.' He glanced at his watch. 'We should all be moving. One ear infection and then home.'

'Sydney,' Harry said. He demolished the last of his bacon and stood up. 'In case you'd forgotten, your daughter's due to arrive at lunchtime. And the plane's due for a service. Yesterday's plan was to return to Whale Beach, then take the plane to Sydney this morning. We've run out of time. To-day's plan is therefore straight to Sydney.'

'We'll have Amy and the baby,' Pippa said blankly.

'Riley'll have to hire a car to take you all home,' Harry said cheerfully. 'I'm having a weekend off. Staying in Sydney until the plane's done. Home Monday.'

'Hell,' Riley said.

'Yeah, I thought you'd forgotten the time,' Harry said, and grinned. 'Now, what can you have been thinking of to make you forget you have a daughter arriving?'

Riley said nothing.

That was pretty much the last Riley spoke for the morning. He retreated into some place no one was allowed to enter. Pippa and Joyce helped Amy and her sleepy baby back onto the plane. Once again Pippa sat in the back with Amy.

Amy was subdued. Pippa tried to keep up happy chat but she didn't succeed.

Even with the headsets turned off, she knew that Riley was deep in silence, too.

There were so many emotions swirling around she couldn't make sense of any of them.

Inviting Amy to stay had problems. It meant she'd have to stay in Riley's house—in the hospital house, she corrected herself—as well, and she was starting to think her wisest path was for her to retreat to her honeymoon hotel and close the door.

Or retreat back to England?

That wasn't going to happen. Not! For she'd fallen head over heels in love with this job. With what Riley was doing. With what Joyce was doing. She wanted to help with a hunger that was deeper than anything she'd ever known.

As a child, on television in some long-forgotten luxury hotel, watched over by some anonymous hotel sitter, she'd seen a documentary. A doctor in South America, treating children's eyes. She'd watched in fascination as bandages were removed and sight was restored, and something had resonated with her at a level she hardly understood. She wanted to work like that, and the desire had never left her.

Nursing in England had been great. She loved her work, and there was always need. But the last twenty-four hours was causing the emotions she'd felt after the documentary to come crowding back.

She *had* to be allowed to be a part of it.

She might have messed with that, she conceded, by allowing last night to happen. And by pushing Amy onto Riley?

Riley was stuck with her and with Amy and her baby as he went to meet his daughter for the first time. This for a man who walked alone? It was a wonder his head wasn't exploding.

What had she been thinking, making love to him last night?

She knew what she'd been thinking. She'd watched Joyce smile at him this morning and she'd thought, Yes, that's how he should be smiled at.

Like he was loved.

And her heart twisted. Love…

Wouldn't it be stupid if it caught her now? Engaged—on and off—for years. Almost married.

What was she thinking? Her engagement had been broken off a little more than a week ago, and here she was thinking of the possibility of falling for another man?

Not just another man.

Riley.

'What's wrong?' Amy asked, and the girl put her hand out and caught Pippa's. 'You look like it's the end of the world.'

She caught herself and managed a smile. The boundaries of friendship and professionalism were certainly blurring. She was a Flight-Aid nurse and she was supposed to be caring for Amy.

'Nothing. Just…dumb thoughts.'

'You didn't really want to drown yourself last week?'

'I… No!'

'I didn't think you did. But you're missing your boyfriend?'

'No,' she said. 'No, I'm not.'

'You're missing someone,' Amy said wisely. 'I can tell.'

CHAPTER SEVEN

FLIGHT-AID had arrangements in place in Sydney so transferring patients, with any delays that involved, could be achieved in privacy and comfort. Collecting patients who'd needed complex medical care and taking them home—back to Whale Cove but more usually back to their Outback homes—was part of Flight-Aid's charter. When they reached Sydney, therefore, Riley was able to take Amy and baby—and Pippa—into a reserved medical lounge and leave them there.

Harry was busy with the plane. Pippa was happy to take care of Amy.

Riley was about to meet his daughter and he was feeling like his head didn't belong to his body.

Pippa. Lucy.

A week ago he didn't have a complication in the world. He wanted, quite badly, to turn back the clock. To head back to Whale Cove, grab his surfboard and ride some waves.

He'd gone to bed last night planning a dawn

start. They'd get back to Whale Cove, drop Pippa off and keep going to Sydney. He'd figure what to say on the way down. How to meet your daughter for the first time?

But he'd figure it. He'd collect Lucy, put her in a hire car and drive her back to Whale Cove. He'd be calm, collected, a guy in charge of his world. A man worthy of being a father?

He'd woken this morning, diagnosed jaundice, knew the early getaway wasn't possible. Then Pippa was suddenly filling his house with people. Acting as if what she'd offered was reasonable.

Pippa.

She was messing with his head. More than it was already messed.

Pippa.

He didn't do relationships. He'd learned it as a kid, maybe even earlier. Keep yourself to yourself and you don't get hurt. For one crazy summer he'd forgotten, and the knife had twisted so hard he'd thought he'd go crazy.

Relationships were for other people. They caused pain.

They'd caused…a daughter.

His eighteen-year-old daughter was about to walk through the arrivals gate.

Three months back, when first contact had been

made, he'd written saying he wanted to meet her. If there was any way she wanted him in her life, if there was anything she ever needed, she just had to ask. No reply. That email seemed to have gone through but his next had bounced— the email address had seemingly been cancelled. He'd gone to England to find her, only to be told she'd gone away, she didn't want anything to do with him. He was her father in name only.

Relationships caused pain.

He couldn't avoid this one.

She was a tourist, he told himself. Curious about a father she'd never met. Checking out Australia and her unknown biological father as an aside.

The huge metal gates were opening and closing as each passenger cleared customs. Reunions were happening everywhere. Families were clinging, sobbing, laughing.

There was a couple beside him. They were in their seventies, and their anticipation was palpable.

The doors opened and a family emerged, mum and dad and three littlies. The elderly lady gasped and clutched her husband's hand. The little family reached them and was immersed in joy.

He did not do this.

When Lucy emerged… She'd be a kid on an adventure, nothing more, he told himself as he'd told himself over and over. Though why her grand-parents weren't funding her to luxury…

Like Pippa was funded to luxury?

Pippa.

It was the sight of the elderly couple holding hands. It made him think he wanted…

He didn't want. He'd spent his life ensuring he didn't want.

The doors slid open.

Lucy.

He recognised her. Of course he did. How many times had he looked at the photograph she'd sent him in her first email? She was thin, tall and pretty, but not like her mother. She looked…like him?

She stood behind her luggage trolley—searching?—and he saw his eyes, his dark hair. And fear.

There was a boy beside her, seemingly arguing that he should push the trolley. He was long and lanky, a kid of about twenty. Worried. He had dark hair curling wildly and olive skin. Then he pushed the trolley sideways and Lucy stepped out from behind.

She was pregnant.

Very pregnant.

She saw him. His picture was on Flight-Aid's website—that's how she'd originally contacted him. He was in his Flight-Aid uniform now so there was no need for red carnations in button-holes. But there was no wide smile and ecstatic wave like he'd seen from most of the reuniting families. There was a tiny, fleeting smile of recognition. A smile backed with fear.

He thought suddenly of Amy. Same age. Same terror.

The thought settled his nerves. Put things in perspective. This wasn't about him. The boy took over trolley duty. Lucy walked out from the barricade then stopped a few feet from him. 'D-Dad?'

'Lucy.' Despite his wish to stay calm, neutral, all the worry in the world was in the way he said her name, all the things he felt about this frail slip of a kid. And she must have heard it because suddenly she sobbed and stepped forward. Somehow he had her in his arms. She was sobbing on his chest, sobbing her heart out, while the kid beside her looked on with worry.

Lucy. His daughter.

He held her close, waiting for the sobs to subside, wondering what a man was to do. Then he glanced over her head—and suddenly Pippa was there, in the background. She caught his gaze and smiled, fleetingly.

Problem? No. She gave a silent shake of her head, waved slightly, backed away.

And it settled him. For some reason it made him feel that he wasn't alone, with a pregnant daughter and who knew what other issues? Pippa would help.

He didn't need help.

He might, he conceded. *His daughter was pregnant*.

Lucy was drawing back now, sniffing, and the boy beside her was handing her tissues. He looked like he was accustomed to doing it. There'd been lots of crying?

'It's great to meet you,' he said softly, looking down into the face of this half-recognised daughter. A part of him? 'You don't know how much.'

'Really?'

'Really.'

'But I'm…I'm pregnant,' Lucy said, half scared, half defiant.

'I noticed that.' He managed a smile. 'How pregnant?'

'Eight and a half months.'

What the…? He gazed at his daughter in stupefaction. She didn't look so far gone, he thought, but, then, some women didn't show as much as others. 'You can't fly at eight and a half months.'

'Mum paid a doctor to say I'm only seven and a half months. I have a medical certificate.'

'Your mother bribed…'

'She wants to get rid of me,' Lucy whispered. 'Because of Adam. This…this is Adam.' She clutched the hand of the boy beside her.

'H-Hi,' the boy said.

'Good to meet you,' Riley said, and held out his hand.

The kid was Eurasian, he thought. And with that, he had it figured.

He thought of the way Lucy's grandparents had reacted to him, an illegitimate scholarship kid from Australia. White trash. Marguerite's father had called him that to his face. And now…for Lucy to bring Adam home, as the father of her baby…

'I'm starting to see,' he said.

'They tried to break us up,' Lucy whispered. 'They even bribed someone at Adam's university to kick him out. They accused him of cheating. They rang Immigration; said he was illegal. We can't fight them over there. Mum says if I keep the baby she washes her hands of me. Grandpa says he's raised one kid he didn't want, and he's not helping with another. So we thought…maybe we could start again here. We were hoping… I was hoping that you'll help us. You said in your email…'

He glanced behind his daughter again, and discovered he was searching for Pippa in the crowd. She'd gone.

He was alone with his unknown daughter. And her boyfriend. And their baby?

Their baby. *His grandchild?*

'Of course I will,' he said manfully, and he took his daughter's trolley and summoned the most re-assuring smile he was capable of. Which didn't feel to him like it was all that reassuring. 'We need to find a car—or maybe a small bus—and head back to Whale Cove. That's where I live. But first there's someone I'd like you to meet. I have a feeling you're going to like her.' He paused and thought about it. 'I have a feeling we're all going to need her.'

Pippa had headed out to the airport pharmacy to replenish her nappy supply. She needed to get her head around supplying an air ambulance; this was an oversight unworthy of a trained midwife but two days' worth of nappies had slipped from her radar. Maybe she'd been thinking of other things.

Like Riley.

So she'd slipped out to buy nappies, she'd passed the arrivals hall and she'd seen Riley meet his daughter. His pregnant daughter.

He looked like he was drowning.

Riley was a man who walked alone—she knew that. You couldn't be near the man without sensing his reserve. And now…he'd been thrown in at the deep end.

He'd be a grandfather.

She almost chuckled, but she didn't.

She bought what she needed, then hesitated before returning to Amy, taking a moment to try and get her thoughts in order.

Riley.

Last night she'd needed him. She'd clung and he'd held. He'd made love to her and she'd lost herself in his body. He'd lifted her out of her nightmare, and in doing so he'd settled her world. She'd woken this morning feeling that all was right with her world, that she was on a path for life.

With Riley?

No. That was dumb. One night of love-making could never make a permanent relationship. But he'd made her feel wonderful, alive, young, free.

All the things he no longer was. His face just then… He had a pregnant daughter and her heart twisted for him.

She'd seen him holding a daughter he'd never met before. A teenager, bearing his grandchild.

He wouldn't walk away. She knew that about

him, truly and surely. He was a man of honour, Riley Chase.

And with that…another twist.

He was so different from Roger. So different from any man she'd ever met. She felt…she felt…

She wasn't allowed to feel. Riley had so many complications, the last thing he needed was her throwing her heart into the ring.

She couldn't. She didn't.

Nappies.

She headed back to Amy, her arms full of nappies, her head full of resolutions. Keep cool and professional. Never be needy again. Support him from the sidelines.

So why was the look on his face as he'd held his daughter etched onto her heart?

Why did her heart still twist?

He hired a family wagon. A seven-seater. Three rows of seats.

The luggage filled the trunk to overflowing. Lucy and Adam didn't travel light. Neither did Amy—babies needed stuff.

Amy was in the back seat, with Baby Riley strapped in beside her.

Adam and Lucy were in the middle seat, holding each other like they were glued.

Pippa was in the front passenger seat next to Riley.

Mum and Dad in the front seat, kids in the back.

Riley was looking…cornered.

She thought back to the evening before, to this same man calmly attempting surgery that was complex and risky. He'd worked through challenges single-mindedly. There was no one she'd rather have around her in a crisis than Riley Chase and that wasn't just because he'd hauled her out of the water. It wasn't just that he'd saved her life.

She'd slept with him last night. It had shifted their relationship to a different level. It could never return again.

Forget last night. She told herself that harshly, but she knew she never could. Somehow she had to move past it, though, to immediate need.

From living on his own, Riley was now faced with living with her, with Amy and her baby, and with his daughter and boyfriend. She thought of his lovely quiet existence and tried to think how she'd feel landed with what he'd been landed with.

Hey. She actually had been landed with it. She, too, was a loner. An only child. A kid who'd learned to like her own company. A woman who'd been independent, whose engagement to Roger had probably lasted as long as it had because she was so independent.

She, too, would be in Riley's house. She was part of Riley's problem—but he was part of hers.

He'd have a bedroom close by hers. That might be a problem all by itself. She needed to put a lid on her hormones.

So what to do?

She was stuck in Riley's house. She'd promised Amy she'd be there.

Riley was stuck as well. Amy needed him to be there.

Riley needed space.

Maybe...

She swivelled. Lucy and Adam could scarcely be any closer. They truly were scared kids.

They had a whole lot facing them, she thought. A baby within weeks. A new country. A future to work out.

A relationship to forge with Riley.

They all needed space.

'Is the house set up for Lucy and Adam?' she asked, loud enough to talk to the car in general.

'Sorry?' Riley seemed a hundred miles away.

'The house,' she said patiently. 'The housekeeper's expecting me on Sunday. She's expecting Lucy today but as far as I can figure, she's expecting a lone Lucy. And she's not expecting Amy. So apart from your room, do we have three more bedrooms—with a single bed apiece?'

'Yes,' Riley said cautiously, not sure where she was going. 'But we can move in a stretcher bed for Adam.'

'A stretcher,' she said disparagingly. 'Lucy, Adam, you guys look really tired.'

'We didn't sleep on the plane,' Lucy admitted.

'So all you want to do is sleep, right?'

'Yes.'

'Then I have a suggestion,' Pippa told her. 'For reasons too complicated to go into right now, we also have one luxurious honeymoon suite in a swish hotel ten minutes' walk away from our house. The suite's paid for until Sunday. Would it make sense if you, Lucy and Adam, had the honeymoon suite until we can set the house up with more beds?'

Silence.

She'd interfered in something that was none of her business, she thought, but this could give Riley space to come to terms with what was happening. And it obviously had its attractions for the scared kids.

'A honeymoon suite,' Lucy breathed.

'King-sized bed. Room service. A bath so big you can swim in it.'

'Compared to a single bed?'

'Hey, it's a pink single bed,' Riley said, sounding affronted.

There was a moment's stunned silence—and then everyone laughed.

It was a good moment. The tension dissipated. Riley's hands unclenched on the steering-wheel and the thing was settled.

Lucy and Adam were to have the honeymoon suite. Riley only had Amy and baby Riley to contend with.

And Pippa.

CHAPTER EIGHT

THEY dropped Lucy and Adam at the hotel with promises to check on them later, then took Amy to the house. They settled Baby Riley in her carry cocoon by the window, showed her the view.

Baby Riley didn't seem impressed by the view but she seemed to soak up the late afternoon rays. 'They'll help cure her,' Riley said. He turned on the heater so the baby could stay in a nappy only, and he tucked the nappy right down so almost all her body was exposed. 'Mother Nature's cure—no medicine needed.'

'It's awesome,' Amy said, gazing around the house in wonder. But Amy was used to living in a corrugated-iron lean-to. Pippa was less impressed.

'How long have you lived here?' she demanded as Amy disappeared for a sleep.

'Six years.'

'Not a picture on the wall?'

'There's a view.'

There was. A veranda ran all around the house

but she didn't have to go outside to see the view. The sea was practically in the house. But still…

'No blinds. Bare boards. And this furniture…it's hospital stuff,' she said. 'Even the beds…. Single, cast-iron, a couple of them are even rusty. How can you live like this?'

'It does me,' he said stiffly, and Pippa shook her head in disbelief.

'If I'm to live here, we need rugs. Curtains. Pictures.'

'You're not living here.'

She stilled. 'I thought I was.'

'I don't think that's wise. After last night.'

'I can hardly go back to the hotel,' she retorted. 'I've promised Amy.'

'Amy's only staying until the jaundice settles.'

'Then you want me out?'

'I'm not saying that,' he said wearily, raking his hair in a gesture she was starting to know. 'Pippa, this whole situation… Lucy and Adam…'

'You think they'll want to stay here?'

'No!' The word was an explosion.

'No?'

'They'll want a place of their own.'

'They won't be able to organise that any time soon. They're your family, Riley.'

'I don't do family.'

'You don't have a choice.' She might as well say it, she thought. It was the simple truth. 'Your daughter's eighteen and she's about to deliver your grandchild. Adam seems even more terrified than she is. They need you, Riley.'

'They wanted to go to your hotel.'

'Of course they did. A nice, impersonal hotel where they can cling to each other without the world intruding—or a single bed and a stretcher with a guy they hardly know.'

'That's what I mean. They don't know me.'

'They don't know you but they need you. They're terrified kids. What was Lucy's mother thinking, to let them go?'

'She'll have orchestrated the whole thing,' he said, anger rising. He dug his hands deep in his pockets and she saw his hands clench within the denim. 'She and her parents. Lucy said she wanted her to get rid of it. When that didn't happen, faced with a granddaughter, a child of Eurasian de-scent... She'll have shipped her off to me. Of all the...'

His face was etched with pain, and she felt ill. For all of them. 'You must have been a baby your-self when Lucy was born,' she whispered, half-scared to probe.

'Nineteen.' He wasn't seeing her now, she

thought. He was staring out at the sea, at the past, at nothing. 'A raw kid. I knew nothing.'

'Enough to conceive a child,' she said, and he gave a raw, half-laugh.

'Yeah. Med student. I couldn't even stop that.'

'It takes two to make a baby.'

For a while she thought he wasn't going to answer. But finally… 'It does,' he said at last. 'I had a…well, dysfunctional family doesn't begin to cut it. Home was never home as anyone else knew it. My mother went from one low-life boyfriend to another, but she liked the sea and there was always a school library at every place we went to, so study and surfing were constants. Finally I got lucky, found some decent foster-parents, got some help. I got into medicine at sixteen. Child prodigy, they said, but obsessive study produces the same effect. Then a scholarship to London. Off I went, delighted to be shot of the mess that family wasn't.'

'Oh, Riley…'

He didn't hear. He was talking to the sea, to something out there that had no connection to anything.

'Marguerite was beautiful, loving, warm, and it blew me away that she wanted me. It was only later that I figured it out. I was straight from the surf. I was big and bronzed and I was Australian.

Her friends thought I was cool and her parents thought I was appalling. It was the combination she wanted. I did know she was in full rebellion mode, but I didn't figure it. That I was simply part of that rebellion. Maybe she sabotaged the condoms, I don't know. All I knew was that at the end of summer she wanted nothing more to do with me. She'll have got pregnant for her own reasons. She never told me.' He closed his eyes. 'To have had a daughter for eighteen years and not know...'

'Oh, Riley...'

'Dumb,' he said. 'I even thought I was in love.' He turned to face her then, and his face was as bleak as death. 'Last night...'

'I'm on the Pill. And I'm not Marguerite.'

'I don't do family,' he said. 'I never have.'

'You don't or you haven't? It seems to me that family's found you. Your daughter...'

'She's my daughter in name only.'

'No, in need. It's not Lucy's fault,' she said, striving to keep her voice even. 'How she was conceived.'

'You think I don't know that?'

'So you found out...'

'Three months ago. An email, nothing more.'

'Then you must have responded magnificently,' she said, quietly but firmly, 'for her to come. You must have told her you care. Three months ago she'll have been five, six months pregnant and terrified. She'll have contacted you looking for options and you've responded with concern. That's what she needs right now. Caring. Family.'

'I'm not family.'

'You are,' she said, and she took his hands in hers and tugged until she had his full attention.

This was important, she thought, for her, suddenly, as well as for him. Her parents had been cold and distant. Riley's had hardly been parents at all. For Riley to be a dad seemed huge. Bigger than both of them.

It was so important she had to fight for it.

'Riley, both our parents messed things up for us,' she said, and she knew she was going where she had no right, but she had no choice. There was something about this big, solitary man that touched a chord.

He'd travelled a harder road than she had, she thought, and he'd come out more scarred. Scars couldn't disappear completely but he could move beyond them. He must.

Riley. She was holding his hands. Strong hands, capable, skilled, loving. Hands that had made her feel…

Don't go there. He didn't want her. Last night was all she could have of him.

Deep breath. He'd been there for her. He'd saved her life.

She was halfway to falling in love with him, she thought. Stupid, stupid, stupid.

He didn't want her, but he was alone. The thought was suddenly unbearable. And with that...

If all that was left for him was his daughter, she'd fight for Lucy. She'd give him a family whether he wanted it or not.

'Lucy is your family,' she said. 'You just have to let her see you care.'

'I don't have a choice. You've landed me with everyone!' It was an explosion of vented frustration and anger. It caught them both on the raw.

Silence.

She could respond with anger. With hurt.

This was too important for either.

'Riley, let's get things in perspective,' she said, somehow keeping her voice even. 'You're not stuck with us. Not for ever. Last night was what I needed to let me move on. It's made things hard between us but not impossible. I don't have a money problem. I need to stay here until Amy goes but that's the extent of it. I would like to stay working in Whale Cove—with you, if that's possible, as part of your team, but that doesn't mean I'm part of your life. I'll get my own apartment. Amy will go back to Dry Gum. I suspect Lucy and Adam will want their own place as well. This is temporary and I haven't stuck you with anything.'

'Pippa, I didn't mean…' He tugged away and raked his hair again. 'Last night…'

'No,' she said evenly. 'You did mean. But we're mature adults. We don't need to let one night mess with our working relationship. And you don't need to see me as the bad guy in what's happened.'

'I don't. Of course I don't. But… You seriously think we can work together?'

And this was the other non-negotiable. He had a daughter. She wanted to work in Whale Cove. 'I want to be a Flight-Aid nurse,' she said, flatly and definitely. 'I'll do whatever that takes, Riley Chase, including never again thinking about what happened last night. Agreed?'

'There's no choice.'

'Of course there's a choice,' she said, and she managed to smile. 'You can walk out that door right now. Pick up your minimal baggage and your surfboard and walk away.' She glanced around the bare walls with distaste. 'It'll be just as it was before you arrived—you'll have left no trace. But I'm staying in this town. For now I'm here to take care of Amy, and if you go then I'll look after Lucy and Adam, too. Because...'

She squared her shoulders and she made herself sound a lot stronger than she felt. 'Because, do you know, I want those ties,' she said. 'I want pictures on my walls. I want mess, baggage, a sense of belonging. Being a Flight-Aid nurse...it's what I've been wanting for a long time and I won't let it go. It feels like home.'

'It's a job.'

'It's home,' she said stubbornly. 'So now... I can see some flowers growing on the cliff face. I have no idea what they are but I'm heading out to pick a bunch. Then I intend to try and make a chocolate cake. I'm the world's worst cook but it feels like the right thing to do. I may only be in this house for a couple of weeks but from this moment on... as long as I'm working for Flight-Aid then I'm home.'

He was called out that night and it was almost a relief.

He wasn't supposed to be on duty. Jake and Sue-Ellen and Mardi were on call over the weekend, but at four in the morning Jake rang.

'Fisherman off the rocks at Devil's Teeth,' he said. 'Wife's only just contacted the police. He was due home at dusk. What was she thinking, waiting this long? Cops have found his gear washed up on the rocks—looks like he was hit by a wave, swept straight in. Sue-Ellen says she can't hack it. Going down ropes, getting bodies… She's hit a wall. She'll do it if you can't, but she's asking…'

It was almost a relief. He'd been lying in bed staring at the ceiling, trying not to think how close Pippa was. Yes, there was a bedroom between them, but that was two thin walls away. If he lay still he could imagine her breathing.

He wouldn't mind betting she was staring at the ceiling as well, and when he dressed and headed out, he found it was a variation of a theme. She was on the veranda, staring out at the ocean.

She heard his footsteps, boots on bare boards. He was in full uniform. It was a bit hard to disguise where he was headed.

'Problem?' She turned and she was wearing a negligee so tiny it took his breath away. Or… maybe it wasn't exactly tiny. It reached her knees. But it clung. The moon was almost full and he could see her body silhouetted beneath the soft silk.

He had work to do. Dreadful work. He couldn't afford to be distracted by a woman in a silk nightdress.

'You want me to come?' she said.

'No need.' He sounded brusque and tried to soften it. 'I'm filling in for Sue-Ellen with the other crew.'

He had a couple of moments to explain. It took Mardi five minutes to get from her home to the helicopter pad. It took him two. He told her and saw her flinch.

'So go,' she said, and he knew she was reliving her time in the water.

'It won't count so much tonight,' he said grimly. 'He went off the rocks at Devil's Teeth, not a calm beach like you did. For him to survive in that water for more than half an hour would be almost impossible and it's been at least eight. There's not a lot to be done but pick up the pieces. Go back to bed.'

'Oh, Riley…'

'Go back to bed.'

How could she go back to bed? She made tea, let it get cold and she didn't notice. Things were happening inside her that she hardly understood, that she had no idea how to deal with.

Riley had stood in the living room in his Flight-Aid uniform, shrugging on his sou'wester, readying himself for what lay ahead. He needed a shave. He didn't look as if he'd slept. He looked big and bad and dangerous…only he was on the side of good.

He was off to haul a body from the sea. It was what he did.

He'd seemed more alone than anyone she'd ever met.

Things were settling inside her. Things she didn't necessarily want.

She was falling in love.

Was that just neediness speaking? The neediness that had seen her reluctant to leave the hospital she'd trained in because that was where her friends were, and friends were the only family she'd ever truly known? The neediness that had finally had her agreeing to marry Roger, because he was her friend, she could have children, she could be part of…something?

The something she'd found here. Riley's team. This hospital. The Outback clinic. Something that called her.

Like Riley called her. Like Riley made her feel.

She was falling…

She'd fallen.

When?

Back in hospital, when she'd woken and seen him at the end of the bed, smiling at her, reassuring her that she was solidly grounded, she was safe, the nightmare was over?

When she'd watched him tease the children at his Outback clinic, making injections a source of fun, a test of bravery that all could face?

When she'd watched him hug Joyce goodbye, his deep affection for the elderly nurse obvious to all of them?

When he'd held her in his arms and blown the terrors away with the heat of his body? When he'd made love to her with tenderness, passion, wonder?

Or when she'd watched him with his daughter, not knowing where to start but wanting so much? Needing so much.

He was on the outside looking in, she thought. For Pippa, who'd been a loner herself, it was an identity she knew too well, and maybe that was what was making her heart twist.

But it wasn't just the one thing making her heart twist, she thought. It was all of him. The complete package. Doctor, lifesaver, father, lover.

Riley.

She thought of his face as he'd left tonight. He knew what he was facing and she knew it hurt something deep within.

Never send to know for whom the bell tolls, it tolls for thee...

Where had that come from? She thought about it, remembering the whole quote. Donne. *No man is an island.*

Riley would like to think he was an island, she decided. He *did* think he was an island. But if you cared as much as he did…

He couldn't stay solitary—it was hurting too much—and if he had to be connected… Could she find a link?

He didn't want a link. Last night shouldn't have happened.

She hugged herself in the chill of the night and gazed out to sea a while longer. She should go back to bed.

Riley was out there, facing a nightmare.

She'd wait here until he got home.

Stupid or not…she'd wait for however long it took.

Like a lovesick teenager…

Or a woman who was starting to see exactly where her home was. Who could heal, and heal herself in the process.

Jake was already in the chopper, and Mardi arrived thirty seconds later. Ten minutes later they were hovering over Devil's Teeth.

One look at the sea told them there was no hope

for a happy outcome. Searchlights were already playing over the base of the cliff. Police were searching the rocks—cautiously as the sea was huge—but the outcome was inevitable

Two hours later, just on dawn, they found what they were looking for and it gave them no joy at all. There was no use for Riley's medical skills. He retrieved the body, then he and Mardi worked to disguise the worst of the damage before they landed on the clifftop.

The family was waiting. The family was always waiting, Riley thought grimly, as he watched the tragedy play out. Ambulances, police cars, desolation, all the accoutrements of heartbreak.

The chopper landed but there was no surge forward. No one wanted to take the first step, to be first to acknowledge death.

And in the end Riley's medical skills were needed. The man's mother-in-law, an elderly Greek lady, collapsed with shock. Riley was about to board the Squirrel but the paramedics called him back. Two minutes later she arrested.

They got her back but only just.

One ambulance left with the elderly woman inside. The second ambulance drove off more slowly, carrying its sad cargo. Finally the Squirrel could leave. Mardi and Jake sat up front. Riley sat in the back and gave in to grey.

Family, he thought.

One death and the ripple effects stretched outward. He'd just watched a wife become a widow. He'd watched a mother-in-law nearly lose her life. He'd watched children and family and friends, all gutted.

He'd watched paramedics and emergency service personnel take on this load of tragedy and carry it with them. Every one of them had a family. Every one of them was exposed to the same kind of grief they'd seen tonight, the type of grief he saw over and over.

Joyce had it right, he thought. Joyce cared for the community as a whole. She put her life into working for the people she cared about, but she'd never let herself be part of that other scary thing, the thing that ripped everyone apart.

Family.

He had a daughter. A pregnant daughter. In a while he'd have a grandchild.

He was thirty-eight years old. The concept of being a grandfather was ridiculous.

It didn't matter how old he was. The concept of being a grandparent was still ridiculous. Terrifying.

And then there was Pippa.

Pippa of the warm body, of the huge smile, of the heart that gave and gave. Pippa who'd given herself to him—was it only last night?

She was back at his house. His home?

Waiting for him?

No one ever waited for him. No one ever would—not if he could help it. His was a solitary world and he liked it like that.

But he had a daughter.

And Pippa was...not waiting?

His solitary world was starting to seem besieged.

CHAPTER NINE

AT DAWN Pippa helped Amy feed a still sleepy Baby Riley. Amy and baby went back to sleep. Exhausted, Pippa abandoned her sentry duty and crawled into bed. When she woke it was ten and Baby Riley was squawking for her next feed.

The jaundice might well recede without the need for phototherapy, she thought, but mostly she thought…had Riley come home?

She padded down the passage and just happened to glance into Riley's bedroom on the way.

No Riley.

Were they still searching, or was he needed at the hospital?

She flicked on the radio to the local news and listened to the account of last night's tragedy.

A drowning followed by a heart attack. In an understaffed hospital that could be enough to keep him busy for hours. Or was he was staying out because of her?

Was she making herself more important than she was?

Keep busy, she told herself. Don't think about him.

Easier said than done.

She helped Amy bathe Riley Junior, encouraged her to feed again then settled them both to sleep in a patch of sunshine.

Lucy and Adam arrived. They'd walked round from their hotel. Lucy's legs were swollen. To fly for almost twenty four hours at full term... There were reasons for regulations.

She settled Lucy on the settee, raised her legs, massaged her swollen feet, working on getting circulation happening.

Sent Adam out for supplies. Made sandwiches. Riley still didn't return.

The place was like home without its hearth. Maybe that was a dumb thing to think but there it was. He should be there.

'I can't believe Dad lives here,' Lucy said, relaxing a little. 'This place is like a barn. Has he only just moved in?'

'He's lived her for six years,' Pippa said. 'But he's a guy.'

'I resent that,' Adam retorted. He was also relaxing—maybe because Pippa was obviously caring for Lucy, and being twenty and the only one to care for a very pregnant girlfriend was truly scary.

'Your dad needs posters,' Amy said, hopping into her third sandwich. 'Pippa rang up this really cool poster shop when I was in labour and next thing we had posters everywhere. The nurses said the poster shop's huge.'

'But I don't have any money,' Lucy said sadly. 'Mum's cut me off without a penny. Adam's broke, too. But it'd be great to decorate this place.'

And Pippa couldn't help herself. She'd run out of things to do. She couldn't just sit still and wait for Riley.

'I'd love some posters,' she said. 'If you order them, I'll pay.'

'Really?' Lucy demanded, astounded.

'I kind of think this house is boring as well. What about surfing posters? That's your dad's thing.'

'My dad surfs?' Lucy demanded. 'Awesome.'

Had Marguerite told Lucy nothing about Riley? Her heart wrenched for both of them, and her resolution built. Family. That meant shared interests. Surfing.

'Let's see what the shop has,' she said.

'Maybe we could intersperse surfing with skiing—it's the same sort of theme,' Lucy said. 'Dad looks like the kind of guy who'd ski.'

He did, Pippa thought. An outdoor adventurer. Living life on the edge. Alone.

He was the kind of guy who'd hang out of a helicopter, who'd risk his life to save hers.

He was also the kind of guy who'd make love to her to take her out of her terror. And mean nothing by it?

She'd told him it meant nothing.

Something was happening inside her she hadn't meant to happen.

It no longer meant nothing.

He spent the morning deep in the paperwork a death by misadventure always entailed. Then, inevitably, he was at the hospital when a car crash came in, and how could he not assist? Finally he was free. He walked back to the house, entering from the veranda the way he always did. Entering his house.

It was no longer *his* house.

For a start it was full of people.

Amy was in an armchair, holding her baby. Lucy was on the settee and Adam was beside her. Lucy had her feet propped up on Adam's knees. She looked even more pregnant today, he thought. The baby seemed to have dropped, settling low.

Uh-oh.

And, of course, Pippa was there. She was seated at the dining table behind a sewing machine, surrounded by fabric. She looked…worried?

His gaze met hers and held. The look she gave him was one of defiance, but her worry stayed. Like…I'm not sure I should have done this.

This?

This would have to be the house.

His breath drew in and wasn't replaced. Breathing seemed extraneous.

He'd left at four that morning. It was now mid-afternoon and it was a different house.

The sea had come inside.

There were huge montages of surf and sky and beach and sun, and smaller montages of skiing, snow and sun.

He saw a series of ten posters of dolphins riding the waves, taken as stills one after the other, from the moment the pod entered the back of the wave to when they twisted triumphantly out as the wave crashed out onto the shore.

And there weren't just posters.

There were cushions. Throws. And curtains! He stared around in amazement. Every window had curtains, great folds of blue and gold, draped from rods with huge wooden rings.

How the…?

'Pippa bought a sewing machine.' Amy seemed the only one not nervous; she was breathless with excitement. 'The fabric shop delivered rolls and rolls of fabric and rings and rods. Adam put up the rods. Pippa's sewed and sewed, while me and Lucy stuck up posters. Adam told us where to put them—Lucy says he wants to be an artist. And Pippa's taught me how to sew curtains. They're easy. She says I can have the sewing machine for a baby present and the leftover material for curtains when I get home. Do you like it?'

They were all looking at him.

It felt…

He wasn't sure how it felt.

There was a part of him that loved it. His house was being converted into a home. More, this was a home designed specifically for him. The views from outside were echoed, but softly, the sunlight diffused, the harsh yellows turned to soft gold. Here a man could take sanctuary. He wouldn't have to head to the surf—the surf had come to him.

He looked at the people surrounding him, Lucy and Adam, tremulous with hope that they'd done something good, Amy, beaming with pride and excitement.

Pippa, looking…wary.

She'd organised it, he thought.

She'd given him a home.

And that was the problem. Did he want a home? Had he ever? He lived out of a duffel bag. He'd never put down roots.

As a kid, his mother had always been dragging him from one place to the next, from one substitute father to the next, from one disaster to the next. Now he made sure his escape route was always open. He'd been here for six years but every moment of that time he'd known he could walk away.

How could he walk away now? He couldn't. Amy was depending on him. Lucy and Adam were depending on him.

Pippa was still looking wary. She looked…as if she expected to be hurt.

Was she depending on him?

'It's fantastic,' he said, as sincerely as he could, and everyone beamed except Pippa.

'It's so cool,' Lucy said. 'It's even better than the hotel. I thought…if we buy a cheap mattress and put it in the spare room on the floor…could Adam and I stay here, too? The hotel was fine last night but here's better. Pippa's been so nice.'

She had been nice, Riley conceded. She'd invited Amy into his house. Her niceness was drawing Lucy in, too.

Nice.

But she was so much more…

'I'm not staying here long,' Pippa said, still wary.

'You'll be here until I have to go,' Amy said, panicked. Pippa cast another sidelong—wary—glance at Riley, and nodded.

'Yes.'

'I want you to be here when our baby's born,' Lucy breathed. 'Amy says you helped with her baby. She says you were lovely. You and Dad both. You know, if you two were here, why do I have to go to hospital? I could lie on the veranda and watch the sea when I'm in labour and I wouldn't have to do any of that scary hospital stuff. And…' Her happiness faded. She gave her father a scared glance. 'It might be better. I… I don't have insurance.'

'You don't have…' Riley was speechless.

'We couldn't get any insurance company to cover me,' she said. 'Not here.'

'Of all the…' He turned and stared at Pippa—who was looking at a half-made curtain. Studiously not looking at him.

His life had been under control until this woman arrived. Since then… 'This is you,' he said.

'Me?'

'It's down to you.'

'How exactly am I responsible for Lucy not having insurance?'

'You're responsible for telling her she can have her baby here.'

'She hasn't,' Lucy said, astounded that he was attacking Pippa. 'It's just… I've heard of lots of people having home births. I thought maybe I could, too. I knew you were a doctor. I knew… I hoped you'd help me. But if you won't…' She sniffed and clutched Adam's hand. 'Adam will.'

Adam swallowed. Manfully. 'I…I expect you will need to go to hospital,' he said, sounding terrified. 'We can figure out how to pay later.'

'But the debt…'

'There's lots of stuff we have to figure out,' Adam said, squaring his puny shoulders. 'Baby first. You first. Let's take care of you. Nothing else matters.'

And Riley looked at his daughter's terrified face, at Adam's terrified response—and he knew his anger at Pippa was totally unjustified.

Lucy was eighteen years old. This was her first baby. She was alone except for Adam, and Adam was scarcely older than she was.

'Will you help us, Pippa?' Adam asked, while Riley fought to make a recovery.

'Of course I will,' Pippa told him, turning stiffly

away from Riley. 'Lucy, Adam's right. There's no need to worry. All you need to concentrate on is welcoming your baby into the world. Do you have any good books? There's lots of stuff to read about what to expect, and it might be fun for you and Adam to read them together. I can borrow them from the hospital.'

'And you should learn breathing,' Amy said wisely. 'I bet Pippa could teach you.'

He was being excluded, Riley thought. Maybe justifiably. What the hell was he doing, putting his needs before Lucy's?

'We'll do this together,' he growled, and he spoke to Adam rather than Lucy because now that Lucy had Pippa and Amy behind her, it was suddenly Adam who was looking the most worried. 'The hospital might be best. I can help you…'

'We can decide that close to the time,' Pippa said, and her tone was suddenly resolute, almost daring him to defy her.

'I hope I'm still here to help,' Amy said. 'Having a baby is awesome.'

'It doesn't hurt at all,' Pippa teased, and Amy giggled.

'It does hurt a bit,' she conceded. 'But then you get this baby at the end of it and it's fabulous. I'm not going to have any more until I'm about thirty but I loved it. Can I help Pippa teach you to breathe?'

'I can breathe already,' Lucy said, and peeped a glance at her father. Who was glaring at Pippa. 'I'm sure I can. Why are you looking at Pippa like that?'

'She's organising my life.'

'I'm not,' Pippa said. 'If Lucy and Adam are staying here, maybe I should go back to my hotel.'

'No,' Amy said, suddenly panicked. 'You promised.'

'I need you here,' Lucy said, sounding even more panicked.

Maybe *he* should go to the hotel, Riley thought, absorbing the fact that he was in a house that had been transformed suddenly into a home—his home—and it was full of people who were depending on Pippa.

'It's like having family,' Lucy said.

And he thought, Exactly.

It was exactly why he wanted to walk away right now.

Another bombshell was about to land.

Amy retired to have a nap. Pippa went back to curtain sewing and Adam put up more rods. Lucy took her father on a tour of the posters.

'I'll pay you for these,' he said, trying to make up for his less than enthusiastic initial response. 'They must have cost a fortune. Plus the sewing machine and the fabric...'

'I didn't pay for them.' Lucy said. 'I don't have any money. Mum said if I stay with Adam then she'd cut me off with nothing. And Adam's an art student.'

'You've come to Australia with nothing?'

'Adam sold his motorbike. That just got us here.'

That made him feel...dreadful. The money itself didn't worry him. He had twenty years of savings, he earned an excellent wage and the overtime in the work he was doing now was truly astounding. But to have Lucy so helpless... And who'd paid for the posters?

'So Pippa paid?'

'It doesn't matter to her. She says she's not your girlfriend, but, Dad, if I were you I'd make a move. She's funny, and she's kind, and she's loaded.'

'Loaded?'

'You didn't know?'

'What are you talking about?'

'I didn't recognise her but Adam did, as soon as he heard her full name. We got the posters delivered. She paid for them over the phone by credit card. She's Phillippa Penelope Fotheringham.'

'It that supposed to mean anything to me?'

'Yeah. It is. I sort of knew about her. She's an heiress. And we know even more, 'cos Adam read a story about her last month while I was getting tests at the hospital. Adam read the glossies while he waited. There was a piece on Pippa. He says her grandfather made millions with some food company. Her parents are socialites—worse than Mum. Even I've heard of them; they're always in the news. But Pippa's not social. The story said Pippa went nursing when she was seventeen. Her family hated it but she did anyway. She's been quiet ever since. The article was about her grandpa saying she's the best of his relations and he's left the company to her. Oh, and she was going to marry the company's chief accountant—that was what the piece was about. You know, heiress finds true love, that sort of thing. I don't know what happened, but what I do know is that she's seriously, seriously rich.'

Dinner was steak and salad, cooked on the barbecue. With Riley thinking Pippa had paid for the steak.

Amy and Baby Riley were asleep before the washing-up was complete. Adam and Lucy headed back to their hotel with baby books. They couldn't get a mattress until Monday but they looked wistful as they left the house.

Riley headed out to the veranda, and Pippa followed.

She stood and watched him for a while. He watched the sea and said nothing.

'You can take the posters down after everyone's gone,' she said at last.

'Why would I want to do that?'

'Because you like bare walls?'

'I don't actually like walls at all. How rich are you?'

'Very rich.' There was no sense in denying it.

'So what the hell are you doing here?'

'I'm not accepting free board and lodging,' she said warily, because there was nothing in his voice to suggest any warmth. 'I'm staying here because of Amy but I'm paying rent to the hospital. The same as you.'

'That's not what I meant. You took the job with Flight-Aid under false pretences.'

'Under what pretences?' she demanded, starting to feel angry. 'Are you saying I had no right to apply? Because there's money in my background?'

'You can apply for what you like.'

'Because I'm rich?' Anger was coming to her aid now, pure and simple. 'I didn't pay for Coral to employ me at Flight-Aid. I was employed on the basis of my experience and my qualifications.'

'It's a plaything.'

'Excuse me?'

'You'll do it and leave.'

'I might,' she said, astounded. 'So might you. I did, however, work in the same hospital in Britain for over ten years. Match that, Dr Riley.'

'What are you doing here?' It was like an explosion. He turned to face her and his eyes were dark with anger. 'What are you playing at?'

'I'm not playing.'

'Filling my house with…what's the quote? A monstrous regiment of women.'

'Like three,' she said, gobsmacked. 'Three!'

'Four. Even Baby Riley howled when—'

'When you gave her her blood test. I'd howl too if someone pricked my heel. Whatever. You're putting her in your conspiracy theory, too? Riley Chase, his life hijacked by women. What about Adam?'

'He'll figure it out,' Riley said harshly. 'Lucy's grandparents…her mother…they're angry with her now but they'll want her back. They'll haul her back into their lives and Adam will be left on the outside.'

'Are we talking of Adam, or are we talking about you?'

'It's none of your business.'

'And neither is my money any of your business. What earthly difference does it make?'

'Why are you working?'

'Because I want to.' She was almost yelling. Almost but not quite. 'I left my job to marry Roger. The deal was that we'd have a long honeymoon, then we'd go back to London and, guess what, I'd find another job. Nursing. I love what I do. Believe it or not, I love it a lot more than I ever loved Roger. And guess what? I've fallen in love again, only this time I've fallen in love with Flight-Aid. With the whole package. With Whale Cove Hospital, with Jancey, with Coral, with nurses who care so much they don't even see the end of their shifts coming. Who see the place as an extension of their lives; their community.'

'That's not—'

'Shut up and let me finish,' she said. 'Because I need to say it. Because I love what you do, too, and I'm not intending to walk away from it. I love the search and rescue component of the job—all the worthwhile things. I sneaked into the hospital when I went for a walk this morning and I talked to Jancey. I know what you did for that family last night. You got his body back so they could grieve, but more. You stayed with them. You talked them through their grief. You made George's body presentable so by the time they saw him he didn't look like he'd died in terror. And then you cared for Maria, you reassured her, you were just there. Jancey says sometimes you doubt that a doctor should be on these search and rescue missions, but everyone here thinks exactly that.'

'This is nothing to do with—'

'Me? Yes, it is, because I'm a Flight-Aid nurse. I've signed Coral's contract. And there's more. Joyce's clinic. Her house-cum-hospital. It took my breath away. I want to be a part of that so much it's like a part of me I didn't know was missing. And I will be a part of it. Jancey says there's two complete crews, two medical teams who cover inland settlements. She says if you and I can't get along then we'll swap teams. Mardi can come to you and I'll go on Jake's team.'

'You talked to Jancey? About me?'

'Everyone talks about you,' she said wearily. 'Everyone worries abut you. They love you, Riley Chase, only you don't get it. You do this loner thing and no one can get near. Jancey says you had the pits of a childhood. Alcoholic mother. No parenting to speak of. One of the older nurses knew your mother and she said—'

'I don't have to listen to this.'

'No, you don't,' she said. 'Like I don't have to listen to you saying my medicine is a plaything. I've come from money and neglect; you've come from poverty and neglect. Either way, we've ended up here. The only difference is that I intend to make here my home. I'll buy an apartment here and you know what? I won't need Adam and Lucy and Amy to make it a home for me because I'll do it myself. Oh, and by the way, while you're busy getting your knickers in a twist, here's something else to get on your high horse about. I'm about to throw more money about. I'm about to set up a trust for Joyce's House. I'll use whatever I need to set it up as an accredited hospital. I'll do it anonymously but I'd imagine you'll find out, so you might as well despise me now. Not for the act. For having the capacity to do it. For what I was born into rather than what I am.'

He didn't speak. He stood staring at her in the moonlight like she was someone he didn't know—and didn't want to know.

'I know how Lucy's mother and grandparents treated you,' she said, her anger finally fading at little as she remembered the bald outline Lucy had told her. She had every right to be angry, but money had messed with so much of her life that in a way she understood his confusion. His emotion. If she could come to this man on his terms…

But there was no way she could. Her money was there, like it or not. She would help Joyce, and she would help other communities, even if it meant Riley looked at her the way he was looking at her now.

'I'm not my money, Riley,' she said softly. 'That's not me. I'm who you pulled out of the water, a woman at the end of her life, a woman with nothing. But one thing this week has taught me is that I only have one chance at life. And Flight-Aid is what I want. But you know what? There's a part of me that wants more. There's a part of me that wants…'

She faltered. She couldn't say it. He was a stranger, standing aloof against the balcony rail, a shadow against the moonlight and the fluorescence of the sea.

He didn't want anything. He didn't want the posters and curtains and the accoutrements of home.

He didn't want her.

What was she doing, being angry with him? She had no right. He'd made love to her only because she'd been needy.

She had to move on.

'I'll stay here for as long as Amy needs me,' she said, making her voice even, almost calm. 'You're stuck with me until then and I'm sorry. I invited Amy here and that was a mistake. I should have got an apartment for her and for me. But moving now…I don't think that's possible without heart-break. So I'll stay here and we'll lead separate lives. On Monday I'll talk to Coral about being ros-tered onto a different crew from you. We'll work apart. That's the best I can do, Riley, but I won't do more than that. I can't walk away completely.'

She closed her eyes and bit her lip. This was so hard.

Just say it.

No.

Yes. Why not?

Why not be honest?

'I can't walk away because I've fallen in love,' she said softly now, but with her dignity intact. 'With Flight Aid, with Jancey, with Amy, with Whale Cove.'

Deep breath. Just say it.

'And I'm very close to falling in love with you,' she whispered. 'Because…there's this connection. I don't get it, I can't figure out why I'm feeling it, but I am. Like we're linked. Our backgrounds.

Something. I'm sorry but there it is. Honesty on all fronts. But I'm a big girl. I've walked alone all my life and I'm good at it. I know you don't want whatever I'm feeling, and that's more of a reason for me to get myself as apart from you as I can without leaving Whale Cove. So for now… you need to put up with posters, put up with sharing your home, put up with people in your life for another week or so. And then… I'm not sure what you'll do with Lucy, but that's up to you and Lucy. For the rest of it I'll respect your right to be alone.'

'Pippa…'

'There's nothing else to say,' she said, and then before she could stop herself she stepped forward, took his hands in hers and stood on tiptoe.

She kissed him and it was a kiss of farewell. She wasn't leaving but she was moving away.

He didn't respond. He didn't touch her.

There was nothing else to be said. She released his hands. She walked inside and she closed the door behind her.

CHAPTER TEN

THEY didn't swap crews. There was no need. Riley simply held himself distant.

Pippa was introduced to full crew membership and she loved it. She loved the work, she loved the remote clinics, and after a couple of days she figured she and Riley could handle a professional, working relationship.

They were both good at holding themselves contained. Practice.

On Tuesday they did a retrieval upcountry—a truck had rolled with three kids in the back. It took all their medical skills to get a good outcome— three kids recovering in Sydney Central—and it felt fantastic.

She could do this.

The house was trickier.

Amy's Jason arrived late on Wednesday night, dusty and worn from hitchhiking for six hundred miles.

'I couldn't wait any longer to see my kid,' he said simply. 'I'll sleep on the beach; I don't need a bed.'

His boss had told him he could take time off to settle Amy and the baby. Amy was so proud she looked like she might burst, so there was now another mattress on the floor. The pair sat and watched their baby slowly work her way through her jaundice. They waited every night for Riley to tell them she was doing well.

Lucy and Adam sat on the veranda, read their birthing books and practised the breathing Amy proudly taught them—and waited every night for Riley to tell them they were doing well.

They depended on him.

Except...they didn't. None of them depended on him. Not really, Riley thought as the week wore on. Because there was Pippa.

She was like the sun with planets spinning around her. She was the life of the house.

She was embracing life like she'd never realised she was alive until this moment, soaking up every moment of this new, wonderful world she found herself in. Her joy was impossible not to share.

Except he didn't share it. Not if he could help it, because it seemed like a void. It seemed a sweet, sensual lure, a vortex that if he entered he'd end up as he'd ended up twenty years before when he'd met Marguerite.

Maybe he wouldn't.

Maybe he wasn't brave enough to find out.

Thursday night. He was on the beach, looking back to the house. Pippa's curtains were left undrawn. The lights were on and he could see them all. They were squashed on the divans, watching television. Pippa had been making popcorn when he'd left. He could see them passing bowls. Laughing.

He'd go back soon. He was necessary in the house. He had to sort Lucy's life. He had to check Amy's baby.

He was useful.

He was…loved?

No. Love was an illusion. Something that happened to others, not to him.

He didn't need it.

He had everything he needed—his medicine, his surf, his independence. He'd set Lucy and Adam up in their own place. Next Thursday Amy would go back to Dry Gum. Pippa would move out.

The ripples in his calm existence would roll to the edges and disappear.

He glanced again at the lit windows and thought he could be in there.

Pippa. Child of money. A siren song.
Stay outside, for as long as it takes.

She knew he was out there but there wasn't anything she could do. He didn't want to be a part of this house.

If it wasn't for Riley, she'd be loving it.

Pippa had gone from general nursing training to Surgical, and then to Intensive Care. Then a case one night had touched her more deeply than she cared to admit. A woman had come in to have her fifth child. During second stage her uterus had ruptured.

Emergency Caesarean. They'd lost the baby and the mother had come so close to death it didn't bear thinking about. Pippa had cared for her in Intensive Care. She'd watched the little family's terror, and their grief for the little life lost.

Five children and each one the most precious thing in the world.

The following day she'd put in her application for Midwifery, she loved it and here was the perfect midwife job. She was caring for Amy with her newborn baby, and at the same time she was preparing Lucy for birth.

Lucy was like a sponge, listening to everything Pippa told her, reading, reading, reading about childbirth, and Adam was almost as eager. But what was more wonderful was that Amy was teaching Lucy. In Amy Lucy had a teenaged ally who'd gone through birth only a week before, who scorned her fears as garbage.

'It's like a teenage antenatal clinic,' Pippa told Riley six days after Lucy arrived, and then winced as Riley grunted a sharp response and went on to do what he had to do.

He was doing exactly that—what he had to do. He was organising life for Lucy and Adam. He was watching Baby Riley's progress. He was making sure Lucy had all her checks; that everything was done that had to be done.

There were enough practical tasks necessary for Riley to deflect emotion.

He'd get his life back soon enough, Pippa thought as the end of the first week neared. In one more week they'd take Amy home and Pippa would have no reason to stay. Then all Riley had to do was sort out a relationship with his daughter, and that had nothing to do with her.

His solitary life suited him.

She had to respect that.

So she'd move out and she'd be more professional than...than... Who did she know who was strictly professional? Who did she know who had no emotional attachment at all?

Riley?

Not Riley. Or not the Riley she knew.

But the Riley he almost certainly wanted to be.

Saturday afternoon. Riley was in the Flight-Aid headquarters, not because he needed to be but because three women and two men and one baby were sun-baking on his veranda. There was no way he was joining them. It wasn't a trap but it felt like it.

They'd be talking babies, he told himself, quashing guilt. There was no need for him to be there.

But there was no need for him to be here either—he could be on call at home—so when a call came he grabbed the radio with relief.

'All stops.' Harry sounded frightened, which, for Harry, was amazing. 'Kid stuck in a crevice off the rocks south of McCarthy's Sound. Tide's coming in, water's rising and he's at risk of drowning. I'm calling Pippa. Take off in two minutes whether you're on board or not.'

They had six minutes in the chopper to take in the information being relayed to them. Harry had met them looking as grim as death and he had reason.

'The kid slipped off a ledge while his dad was fishing. The cliff's not sheer but it's crumbling sandstone, so he slid and bumped, which is why he wasn't killed outright. Just before water level there's a bunch of rocks. He's gone straight down a crevice. He can't get up. In breaks between waves they've heard him screaming. His dad tried to get down and fell—probable broken ankle. He only just managed to get up himself. The local abseiling club's trying to get their members there but no one's available and the tide's coming in. The report was hysterical—seems he's below the high-tide mark.'

It was enough to make them all shut up.

Pippa and Riley sat in the back—this was where they'd operate from if they needed to lower someone to the scene.

Pippa felt ill. Was she ready?

With Cordelia remaining off work she'd been catapulted into the team with little training, but even with the emotional undercurrents, Riley had worked at getting her professional. It had been a quiet week, which was just as well.

She'd learned to operate the winch as Riley was lowered. She'd been lowered herself. She knew the right way to make physical contact with a patient for retrieval. She knew how to operate harnesses.

She knew, in theory, all she needed to make her a viable member of the rescue outfit.

But for a call such as this…

They should have called Mardi, she thought, or another of the members of the second crew. But there'd been no time. Mardi was five minutes away. In the doctor's house, she was right there.

'We're almost there,' Riley said, watching her face, knowing what she was thinking. 'You can do this, Pippa.'

Of course she could. There was no choice—but what was before them took her breath away.

People were clustered on the cliff top. A police car. An ambulance. Half a dozen people.

Even from here she could pick out the father. Someone was holding him back from the edge. He was kneeling, screaming, sobbing.

Another car was pulling up. A woman. Kids.

She couldn't hear the screaming, but she felt it. She watched the woman run to the cliff edge, the policeman hold her back. She watched her crumple.

A part of the cliff seemed to have fallen away, making a rough ledge of rocks at the base, huge boulders scattered randomly. There'd been strong winds for the last two days and the sea was stirred up crazily. The wind had eased now, but the sea was still vicious. It was crashing into the boulders at the foot of the cliff.

Somewhere amongst those boulders was a child.

'He's eight years old,' Harry said over the radio. 'Name's Mickey.'

'If I go down, can we get directions to exactly where he is?' Riley demanded. 'Get the father on the radio. Have someone hold him while he watches but if he saw his kid go he'll be the only person who can pinpoint exactly where he is. Pippa, you're in charge up here. Total control. You know you can do it.'

Did she know? Of course she did. She gulped.

How long did normal paramedics have to train? Not six days.

''Course she can,' Harry said, injecting forced lightness into his voice. 'Or you can come up front and pilot the chopper while I do it. Piece of cake. Just hover and don't hit anything.'

'I think maybe I ought to hold Riley's winch,' Pippa said faintly. 'I'm not all that good at hovering.'

'You never know what you can do until you try,' Riley said, and he caught her gaze and held. 'We accepted you into this crew because you're good, Pippa. Now's the time to prove it.'

* * *

It was the longest five minutes of her life.

She operated the winch while Riley was lowered carefully down to the rocks. Despite what Harry said about 'just hover and don't hit anything', she knew it took huge skill to hold the chopper steady. They were so close to the cliff. The people on the cliff top were forced to move back as Harry took the chopper almost to ground level to give Riley minimum swing as he lowered himself down.

The father's voice crackled over the radio, thick with sobs.

'The big rock to the north of where he is. A couple more yards. Yeah, down there, between that one and the flat one to its side. Oh, God, there's a wave…'

Riley had reached ground level. He was on the flat rock, no longer swinging from the harness. He was on his stomach, peering down. Waves were breaking over the rocks, not much, intermittently, but Pippa thought, How far had the child slipped? How far was the water going in?

'Mickey.' They heard Riley through his headset. He was bracing himself against the wash, trying to see. He'd taken his flashlight down with him and Pippa could imagine him peering down into the void.

'H-help.' It was a child's whisper, choking off, and through the radio system they heard it clearly.

Dear God...

'Can you catch a rope, mate, if I throw it down to you? It's a harness. You can loop it under your arms.'

'My hands... I can't... One of them's behind me. It won't... I can't get it out. The other doesn't... I can't...' There was a muffled sob and then a gasp.

Riley was pushing himself down into the chasm, reaching as far as he could. Swearing. 'Hold on, mate. Hold on.'

Another wave. A scream cut short.

'Dear God...'

He had no choice. He was as far into the chasm as he could reach. The water was swirling round his face, sucking back out of the chasm. There'd be more waves coming.

He couldn't reach.

He couldn't reach!

He was wasting time. There was no way he could haul the child free. If he pushed himself any further, they'd both drown.

There was one choice and one choice only.
It nearly killed him. To ask her…
He had no choice.

'Pippa?' It was Riley, using a voice she didn't recognise. She'd seen the sea wash over him. She'd thought… She'd thought…

'I'm here.' Of course she was. Every sense was tuned to the drama below. She felt like retching.

This was no time for retching.

'He's more than a metre out of reach,' Riley said, and she could feel his anguish. But still his words were clipped and decisive.

'I can't get in—the chasm's too narrow and my chest's too wide. The sea's rising—that last wave went over his head and I damn near stuck. There's only one way we can do this. I'm unfastening the harness. Harry, get onto the cliff and pick up one of the cops—they'll know how to operate the winch. Then, Pippa, I need you to get down here. You're half my size across the shoulders. Do you have the courage to be lowered feet first to grab him? We wait five minutes and we lose him. Even now… Can you do this?'

'Yes.' No hesitation.

'Of course she can,' Harry said. 'Get that harness off, Chase, so we can get it onto Pippa. We're moving.'

To ask her to do this...
  He had no choice. Not if the child was to live.
  But to ask it of Pippa... To ask it of anyone...
  Watch the sea.
  'We're coming,' he called to the child below, not knowing if he was still capable of hearing. 'Hold on, mate. Pippa's coming.'

Riley was on the ledge with no harness. A wave could wash in at any time. Below him was a child, trapped where the sea washed in and out.
  Pippa's fear for them both didn't leave room for any fear for herself.
  Besides, there were things to do. Fear was for later. She had the winch up and was wearing the harness by the time they landed on the cliff top. A burly sergeant ran forward, was in the chopper, was demanding instructions as the chopper lifted off. Harry had forewarned him.
  'I know the basics,' he said. 'Quick run-through?'
  See one, do one, teach one? Pippa had to choke back a hysterical laugh. Surely this was the mantra

at its most dangerous. Harry and Riley had spent a couple of hours teaching her about winching. They'd intended to do more with her but that initial teaching was all she had.

So she'd seen one. She was about to do one. Her life, and Riley's and Mickey's, depended on her teaching one as well.

But needs must and it all flooded back to her, the mantra Riley had drilled in. Steadiness, keeping control at all times, watching the wind, being ready to re-winch at any moment, watching for sway, safety, safety, safety.

The sergeant was good, calm and unflappable, or maybe he was as good at hiding panic as she was. By the time Harry had the chopper centred again over Riley and the child below, he was behind the winch, putting his hand on her shoulder as if it was she who was the trainee.

Maybe she wasn't as good at hiding panic as she'd thought.

'You can do it, girl,' the big policeman said, calmly and steadily. 'We know you can. Pom, aren't you? Never mind, even if you guys are hopeless at cricket, I reckon you can do this. You can sing "Rule Britannia" all the way down.'

She almost laughed.

But then she was slipping out of the chopper, her

feet were no longer touching anything and she was heading down to Riley. She was no longer even close to laughing.

The last time she'd hung above the sea her life was being saved. Now...

Concentrate. Do not sway. Hold yourself firm, steady; Harry and the sergeant can only do so much, you have to do the rest. Head straight down.

Riley was below her.

Down, down—and he caught her. A wave washed over the rock as she landed and she gasped with the shock of the cold water—but Riley had her, holding her, steadying her.

'It's okay. You're safe, Pippa. But Mickey's not and we need to work fast.' He shone the flashlight down and she could see a shock of red hair, a child crumpled into an impossibly narrow crevice.

'Mickey,' Riley called, and there was no response.

'I can't get down to him and he's drowning,' Riley said, and she heard the desperation in his voice. The water from the last wave was being sucked out of the crevice now. How far had it come up?

'I'm watching the sea. At the next break you go down head first with me holding your feet,' Riley said. 'You'll still wear the harness. If the crevice is too tight or another wave comes then I pull you straight out—this isn't about losing you as well. You get the harness under his shoulders or you grab him any way you can and then you get out of there. Old surf mantra—every seventh wave is a biggie, and it seems to be working. Straight after the next biggie and you're down.'

They were working as he spoke, adjusting her harness. He was looping ropes around her waist and shoulders, tying them so he had a rope on either side of her.

'Wait,' he said as she stooped, and it nearly killed her to wait—and it nearly killed him as well.

Then, as the next big wave struck, he held her tight, hard against him, so the wave couldn't move them. His body gave her courage. He gave her courage.

The wave rocked them, filled the crevice, and she thought, Mickey, Mickey...

The wave sucked out again. Deep breath. And then... Riley gave her a hard, swift kiss as the water cleared from around their legs. The kiss was a blessing.

Then she was on her knees, stooping, leaning in...

Letting go.

Riley held her. Her hands touched the side of the

crevice, feeling her way straight down. Hauling herself in. She couldn't worry about the waves—that was Riley's lookout.

She trusted him.

It was so tight—she had to hunch her shoulders as hard as she could to squeeze down.

She had no room to work with a torch and her body blocked the light.

Her hands touched Mickey's hair. She pushed herself further down, fighting to get a hold on his shoulders. He was crammed in hard. Maybe he'd wriggled to get out, wedging himself in further.

'Mickey…'

No response. He'd have been under water, over and over.

His shoulders were hunched forward like hers. In front of his clavicle…a tiny amount of wriggle room.

She got her hands down under, gripping like death.

She couldn't fasten a rope. No room. She grabbed handfuls of his windcheater and tugged. He didn't move. She firmed her hold.

'Pull,' she yelled at Riley, and he pulled and the child shifted. If she could hold him…

She couldn't, he was too heavy, the grip of the

rocks too great. But he was up far enough now for her to get a harness around him. Sort of.

She was holding and tying, keeping the dead-weight steady, and if anyone asked her afterwards how she'd done it, she could never tell them. She didn't know.

All she knew was that she wasn't letting go. If the water came in now she was still holding on for dear life.

The water did come in, but not enough to reach her, not enough either to cover Mickey's head, not now she'd tugged him a little higher. Oh, but he was so limp.

She couldn't think that. She could only think harness.

She had him. She was fastened to Riley. Mickey was fastened to her. They were going to have to rise as one. If Mickey came out without support... if his head fell sideways and caught...if another wave twisted him...

There was no winch on top. Only Riley. Would he have the strength?

Like her, he had no choice.

'Pull,' she yelled, and she felt her harness tighten. She held to Mickey for dear life. His harness held...

And she felt the rocks release them.

She came free just as another wave hit. She

hauled Mickey up and they were out. Riley was holding her, holding Mickey, they were falling backwards against the rocks, simply holding until the sucking power of the wave eased.

And the moment it did Riley was working on Mickey.

There was no room for the niceties of a mask. 'Breathe for him,' he snapped as he set Mickey down on the highest piece of rock so they could work on him. 'I'm on chest and wave watching.'

He still had to watch the sea. If another wave hit, they'd have to stop to hold on. There was no point in getting Mickey breathing again if they were all to be washed back into the waves.

So Riley watched the sea but still he worked, compressing his chest as steadily as if he was in the emergency department of her training hospital. All his focus was on the little boy's chest.

She checked Mickey's airway again—she'd done a fast check and given him a quick first breath as they'd come out of the crevice but now she had time to be careful. She breathed.

If Riley could be steady, so could she. If Riley wasn't panicking, neither would she.

She had her fingers on the boy's carotid artery. Feeling desperate.

A pulse?

It was barely there but she was sure she'd felt it.

'Pulse. Don't even think about stopping,' she told Riley, but he barely acknowledged her. He kept working. When the next big wave hit they worked as one, lifting the child, holding him high, bracing themselves against the rock. Pippa kept on breathing as much as she could. Riley's chest compressions were more hugs during the worst of the wave. As the wave receded Mickey was down on the ledge again and they kept right on.

And then…the little boy stirred. His chest heaved.

He took a gasping, searing gulp of air, and Riley had him on his side in an instant.

He was horribly, wonderfully sick.

And then, amazingly, he started to cry.

Pippa was beside him, on the rock, her face almost touching his. She held him tight as the water washed over the rock's surface. She was making sure his airway wasn't blocked. This time the wave wasn't high enough to be threatening.

How could anything threaten them now?

'You're safe, Mickey,' she said, holding him close as his retching eased. 'Doc Riley's come in his helicopter and we've rescued you. Your mum and dad are on the top of the cliff. The helicopter's lowering a stretcher right now so we can pull you up. How cool to tell the kids at school you were rescued with a helicopter? You just stay still and let me hold you until we get you back to your mum.'

She was amazing.

Pippa…

Riley stood back as Mickey was embraced by his family. He'd done what needed to be done. Mickey's airway was clear, he had oxygen flowing—he was conscious and lucid so there appeared to be no long-term threat from his near drowning. He had a fractured arm and maybe further fractures to his pelvis and ribs but nothing life-threatening. The painkillers were taking effect. He was almost managing to smile.

His mother was holding his good hand and she didn't look like she'd let go any time soon.

His father was hugging Pippa. He didn't look like he was letting go any time soon either. He was sobbing and Pippa was holding him tight, cradling him like she'd cradled Mickey down on the ledge. Soon Riley needed to work on him—he was sure the guy's ankle was fractured—but the man wasn't worried about his own pain. He was only worried about his son.

'It's okay. He's safe,' Pippa told him.

'If not for you… I don't know how we can thank you.'

'Hey, Doc Riley held my legs and watched the waves. It's Riley who's the hero. Plus my gym back in England. How cool that I lost a little weight for my wedding?' She set him back a little, smiling. 'Happy endings. I love 'em. By the way, did you guys catch any fish?'

'I… Yes.' The paramedics were loading Mickey into the ambulance. Riley was helping, but Pippa's conversation had him distracted.

'How many?' Pippa demanded, and Riley blinked. He was thinking of giving the guy some morphine; Pippa was thinking about fish?

'We caught three,' the man managed.

'What sort?'

'Whiting.'

'Oh, yum, are these them?' She seized a fishing basket and peered inside.

'Yes, they are,' the man said, and Riley realised what Pippa was doing. She was dragging him back from the nightmare into a fragment of reality.

Mickey's mother was holding Mickey. The paramedics were making sure he was immobilised for the journey. Riley had his pain under control; there was a moment for normality to resurface and Pippa was making the most of it.

'I guess you guys won't be eating fish for tea tonight,' she said, sounding suddenly wistful. And a little bit cheeky. 'What with having to sit around hospitals waiting for Mickey to get a cast. And you might need one on your foot. That'll take ages. I guess you'll have to eat dinner at the hospital cafeteria.'

The man took a deep breath. He looked at his wife and son. He looked at his other kids—three littlies being held by someone who might be an aunt. He looked back at Pippa.

He looked at his fish and Riley saw the instant when nightmare moved to thought. Pippa had found her reality.

'Would you like a fish?' the man asked.

'I thought you'd never ask,' she said, and she chuckled.

She was incorrigible, Riley thought. She was soaking wet—how she wasn't shivering was a wonder. There was an ugly graze on the side of her face where she'd thumped against the rock on the way up or down. Her knuckles had lost skin.

Her hair was dripping wetly down her back. She looked about ten years old.

But her smile was enough to make anyone smile. To make anyone's nightmares recede.

He'd been comparing her to Marguerite? He was out of his mind.

'You can have all three,' the fisherman said, handing over his basket. 'They're great fish.'

'Really?'

'Really.'

'Oh, and I have a huge family I can feed them to,' Pippa said, beaming, gathering them to her like gold. 'Thank you so much.'

'You saved my son.'

'And you gave me fish.' She kissed the guy, lightly on the cheek. 'It looks like Mickey's ready to go. Let Doc Riley check your foot and then into the ambulance with you. Oh, and do your fishing a hundred feet from the edge from now on.'

'I'm buying my fish from the fish and chip shop,' he growled—but the man was smiling. Everyone was smiling. Everyone had heard the interchange. Even Mickey…

'So can we buy shop chips?' the little boy ventured, and his mother burst into tears. But she was smiling through her tears.

'Happy endings,' Pippa said in satisfaction, heading back to the chopper with her haul of fish. 'I love 'em.'

And when the ambulance moved away, as their chopper rose, she made Riley leave the slide open.

She kept her harness on. They rose and she leaned out as far as Riley permitted.

She had a fish in each hand and she waved good-bye with fish.

Cheering.

Then she settled back into the chopper with her basket of fish on her knee. And beamed.

And Riley…

The armour he'd surrounded himself with for years, the protective barriers which let him want no one, need no one, were gone.

Pippa.

She could have drowned.

He was totally exposed.

She was taking her fish home to her family, Riley thought, dazed. *Her family.*

That would be Amy and Jason and Baby Riley. And Lucy and Adam.

And him?

Yeah. Tonight it would be him.

There was no way he was not being part of those fish.

Mickey was being taken by road to Sydney. He'd need specialist orthopaedic care so there was no medical need for either Riley or Pippa to stay involved. Harry started his routine check of the chopper. Riley and Pippa walked back to the house. They needed a shower. They needed a change of clothes. They also needed to talk, Riley thought, but he didn't know where to start.

What had just happened?

He'd lowered a slip of a girl into a chasm and he hadn't known if they could all survive. As simple as that. If the sea had turned on them…

There'd been no choice. The alternative had been impossible to contemplate—to leave Mickey to drown. But he'd had to ask Pippa to risk her life and she'd come up laughing.

She'd come up talking of fish and of family.

He was feeling like he'd shed something he'd barely known he had. He felt light and free and… bewildered.

He was carrying her fish. He was caught up in his thoughts, so it was Pippa who saw Amy first. She paused and looked across as Amy yelled wildly from the veranda.

'Will you two hurry up? We're having a baby.'

CHAPTER ELEVEN

THEY were indeed having a baby. Lucy was crouched like an animal in pain on the living-room settee. She moaned as they arrived, a deep, primeval moan that told Pippa they were deep into first stage.

'How far apart?' she asked Amy. There was no use asking Lucy anything for the moment.

'Two minutes,' Amy said. 'And she won't go to hospital. She's scared. She just wants you guys. Gee, I'm pleased to see you.'

'But Amy's fantastic.' Adam looked terrified but he gave Amy a sheepish smile as Lucy's moan trailed away. 'She's real bossy.'

'Yeah, well, I know what to do,' Amy said.

See one, do one, teach one. Pippa almost grinned. Then she glanced at Riley and her grin died. He looked like she never wanted a support person to look. Fear was infectious. What was he doing, with a face as grim as death?

'We need to get you to hospital,' he told his

daughter as the contraction eased and her body slumped. 'No argument. I'll phone Louise and take you now.'

'Hey, how about, "Hi, Lucy, great to see you, we brought you some fish?"' Pippa demanded, astonished. The last thing Lucy needed was an implication of fear from her doctor.

But, then, she thought, Riley wasn't Lucy's doctor. Riley was Lucy's dad. Maybe terror was understandable.

So maybe someone else had to take charge.

The contraction was easing. Lucy looked up from the settee and gave them a wavering smile. 'Fish?' she managed.

'Three beauties,' Pippa said, deciding normal was the way to go. Who needed panic? 'Your dad and I caught them from the helicopter. Sort of. While you've been having fun here. But now we're here… Okay, fish aside, it looks like baby's next.'

She gave Riley a sideways glance, trying to figure what to do for the best. He looked under such strain… He'd want Louise, but most obstetricians only worked in hospitals. To have Louise take on her care, that's where they had to go.

'Lucy, love, why don't you want to go to hospital? It's two minutes away.'

'I'm not going to hospital,' Lucy said, in a voice

where the fear came through. 'Please. I don't want to. This feels like family. You guys can deliver babies. I don't want my legs in stirrups.'

Where had she learned about stirrups? The internet, Pippa thought, or old documentaries, pictures of labour wards where obstetricians put their patients in stirrups in second stage as a matter of course.

'Why can't I stay here?' Lucy wailed, and grabbed Adam's hand and held it like she was drowning. 'I don't want to do this. I'm so scared. I want to go home.'

'To England?' Adam sounded terrified. 'We can't.'

'I won't go to hospital. Dad'll help.'

'Lucy, I'm your father. I can't be your doctor.'

'Lucy's not asking you to be her doctor,' Pippa said, figuring she had no choice but to intervene. Riley sounded strained to the limit.

He was right. He was Lucy's father. That had to be his role. Nothing more. But Lucy also needed a professional.

That would be her.

'You all know I'm a trained midwife,' she said, speaking more confidently than she felt. 'The checks Lucy did with Louise on Wednesday showed no problems. Everything's beautifully normal. Lucy, you're delivering a week early but that's fine. I suggest we let Louise know what's happening in case we need back-up. Then we settle down here, with all of us supporting you every step of the way. But if you get exhausted, or if there are signs that your baby's exhausted, then we take you to the hospital straight away and Louise takes over. That has to be the deal. Do you agree?'

'Yes,' Lucy managed, but it was a strangled gasp.

'Cool,' Amy said. 'Do you want us all to stay?'

'Yes,' Lucy yelled, gripping Adam's hand so tight that Pippa saw him wince in pain. 'I want you all.' Then… 'I want my family.'

Family…

Was she still talking about wanting to go back to England?

Somehow Pippa didn't think so.

But she had no time to think about it. Riley was grabbing her wrist as Lucy rode her contraction. 'I'll talk to you outside,' he said through gritted teeth.

'It'd better be quick,' she told him. 'That's a minute and a half between contractions. I need a quick shower to get rid of fish before I can turn into a midwife.'

He wasn't interested in showers. He hauled her

through the door then tugged her along the veranda until they were out of earshot.

And let fly.

'What the hell do you think you're doing?' he demanded, practically apoplectic. 'She's going to hospital.'

'Why is she going to hospital?' His face was dark with anger. She tried to stay calm, but her very calmness seemed to infuriate him.

'It's safer. We need incubators, resuscitation equipment, oxygen, a fully trained obstetrician. Louise is a specialist. Lucy needs the best.'

'You delivered Amy,' Pippa said, striving to keep her voice even. 'Amy didn't deserve the best?'

'Amy was frightened. She didn't know anyone.'

'And Lucy?'

'She has Adam. She has all of us.'

'In a labour ward in hospital? Louise can't work with five of us. Amy and Jason would have to stay here, and Amy's giving Lucy courage. Look at her.' She glanced in through the window—the contraction was past and Amy was making some sort of a joke—making them all smile. 'This is like gold.'

'She could have Amy with her.'

'And Adam?'

'Yes.'

'And you?'

'I don't…'

'She needs you. In the background yes, but she does need you. You're her dad. She wants family.'

'Her family's in England.'

'I don't think so,' Pippa said. 'What mother would pack her eighteen-year-old to Australia to have her baby? Didn't you hear her? Her family's here.'

'You can't make a family in a week.'

'You can if you're desperate. Lucy's desperate.'

'You have no right—'

'To tell her she can have her baby here?' Pippa hauled her wrist away and stepped back, anger coming to her aid. 'Actually, I do. This isn't your house. You've never bought it. You've never thought of it as home. But I'm working for Flight-Aid and I'm renting part of this house. Contrary to you, I've put up decorations. I've bought rugs and made curtains. So this is my home, Riley Chase, and I have every right to ask Lucy to stay. And you know what?'

She tilted her chin, knowing she had no right to say what she was about to say but she was saying it anyway.

'Lucy wants family,' she said, and she couldn't quite stop a wobble entering her voice. 'If you know how much that means… It's the reason I finally said yes to Roger. It's the reason I almost married. I've never had family—not a proper, loving family—and I want it more than anything in the world. I know it's the last thing you want, but that's your problem. For now Lucy and Amy need me. When Amy's gone I'll somehow figure how to get a family of my own, even if it means dogs or parrots, but right now the only semblance of a family I have is here. Lucy needs my help to deliver her baby. So if you'll excuse me, Dr Chase, I have a baby to prepare for. Your grand-child. Family, whether you like it or not. And by the way, you stink of fish, too. Do you want to take a shower and join us, or do you want to go surfing? Alone? While your family operates without you? Your choice. Your choice alone.'

So Lucy didn't go to hospital.

Riley and Jason were consigned to the back-ground.

He and Jason paced. Talked. Lit the barbecue, made a big fire, stoked it. Watched logs crackle and burn and turn to embers.

They'd cook the fish in the embers, Riley de-cided, when the baby was born.

'Did Amy go through this?' Jason asked, awed, as another moan rocked the house.

'She did.'

'I shoulda been here,' the kid said. 'Only she said she didn't want me. Not if I was just going to hang around. Then she went to Sydney and I missed her and I thought…okay, I'll get a job. If that's what it takes. So she went through this by herself. And look at her now. She says she wants to be a nurse. You reckon she could?'

'She'll need to do part of her training in the city,' Riley said, watching through the open windows. Adam holding Lucy's hand. Or rather being clutched by Lucy. Amy was designated coach, talking Lucy through every step of the way.

'Luce, this is brilliant. Pippa says six centimetres, and you remember the book? Every time it hurts you're opening up a bit more. Every time it hurts it means your baby's closer. That contraction was awesome. You're awesome.'

It was amazing for both of them, Riley thought. For all of them. For Lucy had a team second to none.

She had Adam, whose love for her was transparent. She had Amy, who was even younger than Lucy but wise for her years and whose assistance now could, Riley sensed, validate and direct Amy's existence for the rest of her life. And she had Pippa, preparing warmed towels, organising the sterilised equipment she'd sent him over to the hospital to fetch, overseeing her little team…

Pippa looked happy.

She was a woman he hardly knew. A woman of independent wealth, British, straight from the English class system he'd thought he loathed.

He'd made love to her out of need. Her need. But…

As he watched through the window, as he saw her smile, chuckle, give steady encouragement, he knew things had changed. She was wearing jeans and T-shirt. Her feet were bare. Her hair was wet from her shower…

She was beautiful.

He thought of her down the crevice and he felt himself shudder.

'Hey, it's okay.' Jason put his hand on his shoulder, searching to comfort. 'She'll be great. She's got my Amy and your Pippa helping her through. You gotta trust women, mate. Amy says if I toe the line we can get married. How awesome's that? To have your own woman… And Amy…' He glanced in at his Amy. 'I mean…not that Pippa's not great. She is. But it's one woman for every guy, right? Look at Adam. He's in a blue funk now 'cos of Lucy. Look at me. I've even got a job. I'll even come to the city to help her if she wants to train as a nurse. And you…what would you give up for Pippa?'

He and Pippa weren't a couple. He should explain. But there was no time for explanation. Lucy hit full roar in mid-contraction. There wasn't space for a reply and it was just as well.

But the question stayed.

What would he give up for Pippa?

What would he gain?

'You're so close.' The labour had moved fast— five hours from the first contraction and now she was fully into second stage. Youth, Pippa thought. Emotionally, young mums had it hard, but physically they had so much going for them. Lucy was practically shooting this baby out.

'I can see the head,' she told her. 'Adam, do you want to help deliver your baby? Amy, can you support Lucy's shoulders so she can see?'

'Awesome,' Amy breathed. 'Lucy, you're fabulous. Do you want your dad to see?' She hesitated. 'And… Jason didn't see my Riley born. Lucy, would you mind…?'

'You can bring in the whole bloody army as long as they stay up my end of the bed,' Lucy moaned. 'Oooooohhhh…'

'Nearly there,' Pippa said. 'One more push.'

'Get my dad,' Lucy yelled, suddenly desperate. 'I need my Adam and I need my dad. Oooooooow-wwwwww...'

So after eighteen years of not being permitted to do a thing for her, he was there beside his daughter as she gave birth. Riley knelt at the head of the settee, supporting Lucy's shoulders as she saw her baby born, and he didn't feel like a doctor at all.

One more push and the head slipped into view. Pippa was there, with warmed towels, warming the tiny head even before the shoulder came out.

'Stay underneath with the towels,' she told Adam as a last massive contraction ripped through.

And so, as Amy and Riley held Lucy up to see, Riley's grandchild slipped into the world, to be caught by Adam, who looked like the sky had opened to reveal the secret of the heavens.

'What...? What...?' Lucy gasped as Adam gazed down in awe and Pippa did a fast check of the baby's airway, making sure that everything was in working order. 'What is it?'

'Look for yourself,' Riley growled, and felt a bit...a bit like Adam looked.

'I have a boy. Oh, I have a boy!' Lucy burst into tears. And then... 'Ohhh...'

For Pippa was quietly directing Adam, showing

him what to do, and Adam was settling his tiny son onto Lucy's breast.

The tiny baby hadn't made a sound, but his eyes were wide open, wondering, and now…

He stirred and wriggled, skin against skin against his mother's breast. Without prompting, Adam carefully guided the little mouth to where it needed to be.

He found what he was looking for. His tiny mouth centred—and Riley's grandson found his home.

And Riley's world shifted once more. He glanced up and saw Pippa's eyes filled with unshed tears—and maybe his were the same.

His grandson had arrived into his family.

His family.

It was almost midnight before they ate their fish, and for all of them it was a truly memorable meal.

Jason and Amy cooked the fish. Pippa produced a salad. Riley found some chocolate biscuits.

You could spend thousands on a meal and not get better, Riley decided. They were all out on the veranda. The boys had lifted Lucy's settee, Lucy and all, out where she could see the luminescence of moonlight off the ocean. She ate her fish and her chocolate biscuits—she was starving.

She had a little name discussion with Adam, then she snuggled down to sleep, her baby beside her.

Adam watched their baby as if it was only he who stood between his son and all the threats of a dangerous outside world.

Adam had grown ten years in this afternoon, Riley thought. He'd make a good partner for his daughter.

He'd be a son-in-law to be proud of.

Part of a family to be proud of?

Until the meal was ended there were things to do, but now… Amy and Jason were snoozing on the sun loungers. Soon they'd roll into bed. Both babies were asleep.

'I'm going to the beach,' Pippa said abruptly. She'd been carrying stuff into the kitchen. Now she came out and walked straight down the steps to the garden. 'See you later.'

He let her go. He was feeling…discombobulated.

His grandson was right beside him. He was thirty-eight years old and he felt a hundred.

He was watching Pippa in the moonlight.

She was wealthy. English. Good family.

He was a guy from the wrong side of the tracks. He was a guy who'd had a kid at nineteen, who was a grandpa at thirty-eight.

Pippa reached the gate leading down to the beach

and he realised with a shock that she was no longer wearing jeans. She was wearing a sarong.

He'd seen it before. She wore it over swimmers.

'You're not going swimming?'

'I won't go out of my depth.'

'What about night-feeders?'

'I've painted my nails with Anti-Chew. Precautions R Us. You going to sit on the veranda for the rest of the night…Grandpa?'

Grandpa… The word still had him stunned.

She chuckled, she tossed her towel over her shoulder and she headed down the cliff path.

Grandpa.

Family.

Pippa.

CHAPTER TWELVE

CONTRARY to what she'd told Riley, Pippa had no faith at all in Anti-Chew. She consequently had no intention at all to bathe in the ocean.

There was, however, a rock pool at the edge of the cove. It was a naturally formed ring of rocks. At high tide the waves washed over it, meaning it was full of clear seawater. At low tide—now— there was an almost eighteen-inch rim of rock. The pool was five feet deep at the most. There was no way night feeders could get in. It was safe and she needed to swim.

It had been one incredible day. First Mickey. Then Lucy's baby. And watching Riley...

His face had been changing all day. It was like he was fighting some desperate internal war, and he wasn't winning.

She'd fallen in love with him.

How had she ever thought she could marry Roger? Oh, if she had...

She shuddered and dived into the rock pool. The

water was cooler than she'd thought it would be, fresh from the sea, and she shuddered again.

She decided to swim and stop thinking.

The thoughts wouldn't stop.

Riley.

Could she stay on at Whale Cove if he didn't want her love?

He'd made it plain that he didn't. Lucy was hauling him into family whether he liked it or not, but to have a needy, besotted nurse at his side as well…

'It's not going to happen,' she told herself, and then she thought of how she'd felt that morning, on the rock, clinging to Mickey, clinging to Riley.

Feeling like…if she died now at least she'd known Riley. At least she'd had one night.

'I want more nights,' she said out loud, and started doing laps, up and down the length of the rock pool. She was tired to the bone, but she also knew she wouldn't sleep. She might as well exhaust herself properly.

What would she do?

She wanted to stay here. She wanted to be part of this community, this job, but how much was the job and how much was Riley?

Tonight had been magic. Friends, family, kids, babies, barbecues at midnight, no clear delineation between work and home, saving Mickey, waving her fish from the helicopter, loving Riley...

She almost sobbed, only it was hard to sob when she had her head down, swimming hard. She closed her eyes and let the darkness envelop her.

Something touched her foot.

She pretty near had a palsy stroke. A night feeder...

She whirled in the water to face whatever it was, expecting teeth—and two hands landed on her shoulders, holding her up. Riley's voice growled into the night.

'I thought you'd have learned your lesson about night swimming.'

She'd whirled too fast. She had a mouthful of water. She spluttered and choked and it took a couple of moments before she could breathe properly, let alone reply. But finally...

'If I'd died of fright,' she said, with as much dignity as she could muster—which actually wasn't very dignified when she was still spluttering and when his nose was only inches from hers—'it would have been your fault.'

'No deaths today,' he said gently, in a voice she didn't recognise. 'Only life. First Mickey. Then Lucy's baby.'

How to answer that? She fought for something innocuous. Something safe.

'Did...did they decide what to call it?' She was practically gibbering.

'It seems they thought of calling him Riley,' Riley told her, gravely. 'Only there's a bit of a run on the name. They're moving to William instead.

'I like William,' she said, and then managed a tentative smile. 'Do you? Papa?'

'Papa,' he said blankly.

'Papa. Or Grandpa? Grandfather? Sir? Hmm.'

'You want to get ducked?'

'Gotta be one,' she said, recovering courage. 'There's no getting away from the fact that you're a grandpa.'

'I don't think I want to get away,' he said, and there was enough in that to give her pause.

'You don't do family.'

'I haven't done family.'

'You don't want—'

'I haven't wanted. Until now.'

She paused. She was suddenly acutely aware that Riley was holding her up. They were in the deepest part of the pool. He could stand up. She couldn't.

She was at a disadvantage. She needed to put her feet somewhere solid, but Riley was holding her and not letting her go.

'I thought you might die,' he said, almost conversationally, and instead of moving to shallow water where a girl could set her legs down, he swung her up into his arms. 'Today with Mickey... You risked your life and, more than that, it was me who asked you to. You just...did it. And then tonight you delivered Lucy's son. You've made Amy happy. You've made Lucy happy. You saved Mickey. Wherever you go, life follows. And you know what? I've been sweating on an accent and on money and on past history, and they haven't let me see what's before my eyes.'

'Golly,' Pippa said, which ridiculous but she couldn't think of anything more sensible to say. 'I don't think I'm that good.'

'And you're practical, too,' Riley said, ignoring her interruption, and she heard his smile. From where she was she couldn't see his face.

She could feel, though. She was enjoying feeling. She was starting to enjoy feeling very much indeed.

'Even at the cliff this afternoon,' he said, almost conversationally, 'I was worrying about Mickey. I was worrying about practicalities, transport, shock, you, even about dry clothes—and suddenly you were organising fish. You had your priorities. Free fish. That's a woman in a million, I thought.

And then you know what else I thought? I thought I really want to kiss you.'

'Really?' she said, cautiously. Something inside her was starting to feel…good.

'Really.' He tugged her higher then, and he kissed her. He was shoulder deep in water. He was holding her hard and he was kissing her as she wanted to be kissed. As she ought to be kissed.

A girl had a right to be kissed like this.

'So…so what…?' she ventured when she could finally get a word in. 'What made you think…you might want to kiss me?'

'Adam,' he said. 'And Jason.'

That didn't make sense. She waited, hoping for an explanation, and finally it came. After the next kiss.

'They're sitting on my veranda like two smug old men—fathers!' he told her. 'And they're looking at me like they're sorry for me. And you know what? They're right. I'm sorry for me.'

'You don't sound very sorry.'

'That's because I'm planning,' he said. 'I have a plan.'

'A plan.'

'I'm not exactly sure how I feel about you being rich.'

'You're not exactly poor.'

'Shut up, my love,' he said. 'I need to tell it like it is.'

'Okay,' she said—happily now, for how could she stop the wave of happiness engulfing her? She had no intention of trying.

'I love our house,' he said, and she blinked. Our house. This wasn't the sort of declaration she'd been expecting.

'It's a great house,' she managed.

'It's a magnificent house. And now you've decorated it...'

'I can do better, given time.'

'That's just it. I'm worried. The hospital offered to sell it to me last year and they gave me a figure. If the valuer sees it now, with its curtains and its posters, it'll double in price. I'm parsimonious. Just think of the extra fish and chips we can have if I buy the house now.'

'You want to buy the house?'

'I do,' he said. 'Because I've been thinking... If I buy us a house...no, if I buy us a *home*...then anything else is icing on the cake. No matter what either of us earn, no matter what you decide to do with your fortune, my pride is catered for. Oh, and I might want to start an Amy nursing-training scholarship fund as well, but I've been thinking I might invite you to join me. My pride could take that.' He smiled. 'My pride might even enjoy it.'

'Your pride?' She was still being cautious. He was circling the issue, she thought. She thought she knew where he was heading, but a girl had to make sure. 'You're saying you want us to fund Amy—and you want us to stay being housemates?'

'No.'

'No?'

'Well, only so much as… Are you housemates when you're married?'

'Married.' The word took her breath away.

'If you want to be,' he said. 'I want to marry you more than anything else in the world—but it's your call.'

'But…why?'

'Because I love you,' he said simply, and he did set her down then, moving so they were waist deep in water and he could take her hands and gaze down at her in the moonlight. 'Pippa, this morning… If I'd lost you, I couldn't bear it. I won't ever ask you to risk your life again.'

'Of course you will,' she retorted, diverted. 'We both will. It's what we do. We rescue people.'

'How about ourselves?'

'You mean…' She tried to think it through. She was feeling so happy she felt like she was floating, but she needed to make her fuzzy mind focus. 'You rescue me and I rescue you right back?'

'That's the plan,' he said, softly and surely in the moonlight. That's the dream. 'For as long as we both shall live.'

'That sounds extraordinary,' she whispered.

'Is that a yes?'

She made herself pause. She made herself consider.

Once upon a time she'd agreed to marry Roger. That had taken her years to decide and she'd still made a mistake.

But Riley...

She looked up into his lovely anxious face and all the answers, all the years to come were written in his gaze.

He loved her. From this day forth...

Her Riley.

But...er...

A thought had occurred. Something important.

'You're a grandpa,' she said, suddenly astringent. 'If you're a grandfather and I marry you...I will not be Granny.'

'I've thought about that, too,' he said, sounding suddenly smug. 'Just now. When you called me Papa.'

'You have?'

'I'll be Poppa,' he said. 'I like it. I know I'm young but the word has a certain cachet. And you're Pippa. Poppa and Pippa. A matching pair. How about that for a plan?'

'Oh, Riley.'

'Is that a yes?'

'I believe it is,' she said.

'I believe I love you—Pippa,' he said.

'And I love you—Poppa,' she murmured, and he laughed and hugged her hard—and then she wasn't able to say anything at all for a very long time.

And almost twelve months to the day, to Pippa and to Riley, one baby. Any minute now…

On the veranda of the house overlooking Whale Cove Pippa crouched on a settee and moaned. A lot.

She had the right.

Jason and Adam were in the back yard, firing up the barbecue. Organising fish. Since saving Mickey there always seemed to be fish arriving at this house. The fishing community was big and the locals remembered. *'For our Doc and our Pippa.'*

Our Pippa.

But Riley wasn't noticing fish now.

Lucy and Amy were taking turns to coach.

Jancey was in the background. A woman had to have a professional there.

Pippa's fingers were clinging so hard to Riley's that he might end up scarred.

But Riley wasn't noticing his fingers either.

'It's coming,' Amy said. Six months into nursing training, she was already an expert. 'Pippa, you're nearly there.'

'We can see the head,' Lucy breathed. 'Hold her up, Dad, so she can see for herself. Pippa, one more push.'

'You can do it,' Jancey said.

A monstrous regiment of women.

Riley remembered the quote. He almost grinned. Jancey and Amy and Lucy—and at the centre his own wonderful Pippa. How had he ever thought...?

But then...

'Push,' Jancey ordered. 'Biggest one yet. Keep going. Again. Go, girl. You rock. Lucy, Amy, hold Pippa so Riley can catch his baby.'

He couldn't sit around thinking all day. He had work to do.

He had to disengage those fingers.

'Push,' he told his beloved. He kissed her hard and fast and then he put her into the care of Lucy and Amy. Her family. His family.

And he moved to where he needed to be.

The head… It was certainly coming. 'Push.'

'Don't tell me what to do,' Pippa yelled. 'I'm pushing.'

'Push harder.'

'I'm… Oooooohhhhhh.'

And there she was, sliding into the outside world. Caught by her father. Held like she was the most precious creature in the world.

His daughter.

'What…? What…?' Amy and Lucy were supporting Pippa so she could to see her baby. Jancey stood back with a smile wide enough to split her face. With this family, what need for a midwife?

'We have a daughter,' Pippa murmured, awed. 'Oh, Riley.'

'I have a sister,' Lucy sniffed, jubilant. 'Oh, wait, that means William has an aunt. Our family's getting bigger and bigger.'

'As it should,' Riley managed, so choked he could scarcely speak. 'It's perfect. She's perfect.'

And he moved, carrying his brand-new daughter so that he could kiss his wife. His Pippa. His love.

And as Pippa cradled her newborn, as he gathered her into his arms, as he held her close, and as they felt this new little life between them, he accepted what he knew for sure.

'We have the perfect family.'

'It might get bigger,' Pippa whispered, dazed.

He kissed her again and he smiled and looked up at the people around them.

'A bigger family sounds great to me,' he told her. 'Just as long as you stay at its heart. My Pippa. My love. My wife.'

* * * * *

February

THE DOCTOR'S REASON TO STAY	Dianne Drake
CAREER GIRL IN THE COUNTRY	Fiona Lowe
WEDDING ON THE BABY WARD	Lucy Clark
SPECIAL CARE BABY MIRACLE	Lucy Clark
THE TORTURED REBEL	Alison Roberts
DATING DR DELICIOUS	Laura Iding

March

CORT MASON – DR DELECTABLE	Carol Marinelli
SURVIVAL GUIDE TO DATING YOUR BOSS	Fiona McArthur
RETURN OF THE MAVERICK	Sue MacKay
IT STARTED WITH A PREGNANCY	Scarlet Wilson
ITALIAN DOCTOR, NO STRINGS ATTACHED	Kate Hardy
MIRACLE TIMES TWO	Josie Metcalfe

April

BREAKING HER NO-DATES RULE	Emily Forbes
WAKING UP WITH DR OFF-LIMITS	Amy Andrews
TEMPTED BY DR DAISY	Caroline Anderson
THE FIANCÉE HE CAN'T FORGET	Caroline Anderson
A COTSWOLD CHRISTMAS BRIDE	Joanna Neil
ALL SHE WANTS FOR CHRISTMAS	Annie Claydon